WASTFLAND

Through Dust to Freedom

KAJA GRIL

Weyn
Ixah
Virigor
Generator
Mitg
Sparrowtown
Vormir
Tjos
Dowak

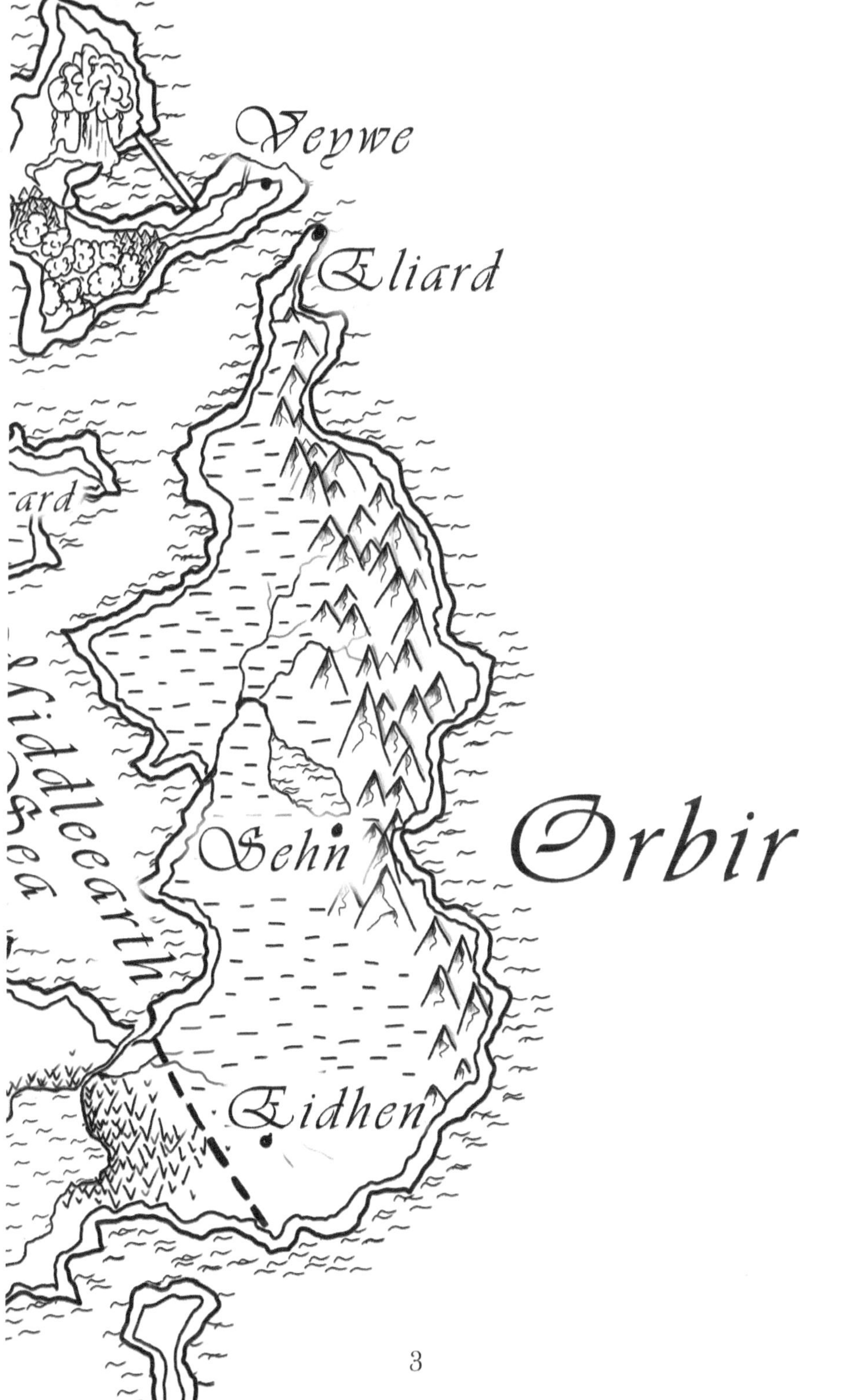

Veywe
Eliard
ard
Middleearth
Sehn
Orbir
Eidhen

Wasteland

CHAPTER 1

A Sea of Dust

Wasteland
CHAPTER 1: A Sea of Dust

She sighed and leaned her aching arms on the window. It was dark outside and a light breeze was cooling her warm cheeks. The red moon was watching over the once sky blue lake. Since the incident, the world has become a wasteland. The forests, which used to be lush and green, are now turning a sickly yellow from the decay. There is no sight of life anymore. The world is cold and the sky is filled with red dust. People are slowly dying, one by one. The wind got stronger and before she managed to close the window, the room was filled with dust, attacking and choking her profusely. Her eyes watered as she ran out of her room, gasping for air. The hallway was ice-cold. Nobody else seemed to have trouble sleeping. She looked around and walked to the staircase leading to the main door.

„Where do you think you're going, young lady?" A dark figure stopped in front of her.

„I need fresh air."

„Well you won't find it outside, that's for sure." The manly voice laughed. It was Cain, her supervisor.

„Girls aren't allowed to be outside at this hour."

„And guys are?"

„Well, men are stronger, faster, smarter and certainly more re-sponsible." A sudden feeling of belligerence washed over her, as he resented women/girls as he called them.

„What makes you say that?" She replied arrogantly.

„A man never gets pregnant and ruins his partner's life." He laughed again. She restrained her urge to not punch him in the throat. His girlfriend got pregnant once. By his words -ruined his life. Of course, he left her alone and now he brags about it to every-one in the home.

„Okay." She said and swallowed. She pushed all the feelings deep inside her mind. She was used to it.

She turned around and stormed her way back to her room. The red dust had now settled down all over the floor and her bed. She sighed at the sight of the old sad room and leaned on the window again. She watched Cain drive away across the red sea of dust. He never spent the night in the home. She dragged her aching body from the window downstairs again, to which there was a small wooden cabinet, full of creepy-looking gas masks. She took the one with her name on it and wiped the glass with her shirt. As she put it on, she was greeted with a foul smell. It was old and probably unsafe too, but it was the only one she had. She grabbed her coat and pulled the handle of the large metal door.

The night was cold and fresh. She came to see the stars. She did every night since the red dust appeared, but every day she saw them less and less until one day they were gone. The moon is just a red circle flowing on the sky, haunting everyone whoever looks at it. She almost forgot the feeling of grass tickling her feet or the water splashing her while she swam. Her memories were corrupted thanks to her experience at the camp. But she won't think about the camp. Not anymore. It's far behind her in Ijos now. Her bulky boots lifted up a cloud of dust with every step she took towards the brown-tinted lake. He was waiting there for her already. His grey eyes reflected in the glass of his green mask. She didn't see it but she could feel his grin cracking wider as he saw her. His blonde hair was shimmering in the red moonlight and his hands were just as cracked as hers were. She returned the smile, even though he couldn't see it.

„I see you're ready." She said with a wave.

„I see you're late. Again." He grumbled.

„Yeah. I met Cain."

„Marvellous." He sighed sarcastically. „Did he cause any trouble?"

„No. He wasn't drunk today." She replied with a frown on her face.

„How's your bruise?" He touched her wrist. It was mesh of purple and blue skin from the other day when Cain drunkenly pushed her down the staircase. Without saying a word, they got up and started walking along the small lake. The waste was almost overflowing the banks. What was once clear turquoise water had now been transformed to a dump of oil, radioactive waste and other trash. You

Wasteland

could almost hear the earth howling from the pain of acid eating it up.

The sad lake didn't stop them. They walked past it a hundred times; to work, for walks, to the city. They just stopped caring. They weren't headed to the lake anyway. They walked across what looked like an endless ocean of dust. The wind carried tons of it with it, brushing against the masks that were keeping them from their demise. She looked over to him, and Dust surprisingly looked better than usual. Underneath his light, slightly oversized shirt, he barely looked sick. He suffered from God-knows-what. Sometimes he would just collapse in the middle of nowhere. She had an unfettered hatred for the world, for all the pain it brought him. His name is somewhat ironic, but it was fake anyway, as they all had fake names. Cain thought it would be much safer that way. You never know how people will use your name against you. The poisonous dust has become the norm. The radioactive waste brought many diseases, unknown to the world. Unable to cure them people were dying and being buried in mass graves. When the cures were finally released, they were on the expensive side. She glanced at Dust again. His arms and legs were thin. The black T-shirt hung from his limp body, waving around him like a flag. He was wearing dark green army pants and black boots - just like her. They all had the same clothes in the home.

„Left or right?" Dust asked, looking at her over his shoulder.

„How promising do they look?" She said trying to make out the outlines of the mountains in the distance.

„The usual."

„Let's flip a coin?" She said, as she reached for her pocket.

„Heads means left." He pointed to the left side.

„Deal." She put the coin over her thumb and launched it high in the air. It landed safely in her palm. She flipped her hand and put the coin on his stretched out hand.

„Tails!" She yelled. „You lost!"

„Hey! We didn't bet! He said and ran after the running girl.

„Nothing." She sadly said to the approaching figure.

„It's all red again." She sighed and sat down on a rock.

„It's okay. We'll find it next time." He tried to seem cheerful and sat down next to her. Her disappointment grew more this time. She had hoped to catch a glimpse of the shimmering silver moonlight. He tried to cheer her up.

„Stars won't just disappear, Envy. We'll find a mountain high enough one day, I promise." She forced a sad grin on her face and hugged her knees. Staring off to the distance, a slow steady wind started to blow.

„I think we should go." He said and held her shoulder.

„Wait. The sun will rise soon."

„So will Cain. We don't need more trouble." She slowly stood up and started walking down the hill. She caught the first red ray of sunshine over her shoulder before it disappeared behind the mountain.

CHAPTER 2

Captivity of The Soul

CHAPTER 2: Captivity of The Soul

The sun was edging over the skyline when they returned. Cain was just entering the building. They both quietly looked at each other. If he finds out they were out all night again they will have to leave. Maybe it seemed like the better option, but they had shelter, food and water there. Cain was kind enough to let them stay out of concern for their safety. They both knew that very well. They looked through the window into the hallway. Cain was headed to the girls section.

„You climb up and I'll drop off our masks." Dust said quietly." She just nodded and dug her fingers into the old decaying wall. Luckily, her room was on the first floor. She just has to climb one window, and she will be there. Taking a few deep breaths, she launched herself up to grab the window sill. She knew where to put her hands and legs. She's done it many times it's been burned into her muscle memory. But today she was frail and worn out from working every day. She grabbed the sill of her window and struggled to pull herself up. Her body ached from standing all day, and was just fed up with the place. She wanted freedom.

Leaping from her wide-open window on the bed was obviously a horrible mistake. A huge cloud of dust filled the room, forcing Envy to take cover with a bed sheet. A loud knock on the door startled the bed sheet from her grasp.

„God, Envy. What were you doing in here?" Said Cain in an arrogant tone.

„Obviously not cleaning." She smirked.

„Won't you ever learn not to talk back?" He was half yelling at her. „Come here." She slowly rose from her bed, knowing too well what kind of punishment awaits. He abruptly grabbed her hand and slammed it against the doorframe. Her eyes welled up with tears but she stood strong. She was stronger. She was unbreakable. She clenched her fist and bit her lower lip.

„That'll teach you." He yelled loudly at her and slammed the door when he left.

That day wasn't the best for Envy and Dust. They both went to work in an oil farm. Every day. They both returned after 11 in the evening. Every day. They were both beaten by the guards. Like everyone else. But that night when Dust was waiting by the lake, she didn't show up. When he knocked silently on her door, she didn't answer. She was busy with her thoughts. Who was she? She wasn't Envy. She was Jade. Her real name was Jade... And Dust wasn't Dust. „Who is he anyway?" She quietly asked herself. The knocking interrupted her only the third time.

Dust was standing in her door frame, looking at her cheeks shining in the red light coming from the window behind her. She had obviously been crying. His stomach twisted churned at the thought of her in pain. But even now she looked pretty. Her brown hair was a bit curled and looked soft like silk. He had to hold back from reaching to her and stroking it. He wanted to make her pain go away. He wanted to help. But he knew it was their fate to stay here. At least until they find a mountain high enough. He looked at her from head to toe, noticing her dove white nightgown. She looked pretty even with scars all over her body. Her soft blue eyes were shining from tears in them. He always felt warm when looking at her, but not to her knowledge.

„Can you stay the night?" Envy asked him. Of course, he wouldn't deny for a good friend. He sat down on a chair on the other side of the room.

„Who are you?" She asked quietly.

„I'm Dust. You know me already." He replied confused.

„My name is Jade." She immediately covered her mouth upon realising the horrible mistake she had made. He could be working for the Leader. After elapsing an awkward pause, he spoke.

„I'm Charon." He looked down at his feet and clenched his fist. He waited for her to speak but she didn't.

„Jade is a lovely name." He blushed.

„Thank you. Yours too."She said back quietly.
They both knew they couldn't call each other by real names, albeit was a pity. They both liked their names. She quickly fell asleep but

he couldn't. He wanted to take her away from the pain in the dark oil farms. He wanted to take her away to see the stars. To live high up in the mountains. Where the sky is clear and the air is clean. Where the sun is still yellow instead of bright red. But he couldn't. This was the only place where they could survive, with all the food and water they had there. Even if it was just soggy bread and warm brown puddle. And a place to hide from all the waste. They called it the home. It was a large grey building with many windows, rooms and halls. Each of the oil farm workers got their own room. It was simple. A thin mattress laying on the floor, a wooden chair and a desk was all they had. They couldn't sleep in the same room to prevent any rebellion. Each day they woke up before dawn. Each day they formed a clean line of people wearing gas masks to the oil farm. Each day was the same as the last. They were all wearing the same clothes. Once in the farm they chained their hands into steel chains. The gasses leaking from the pipes inflamed their lungs. They worked until the sun set behind the mountains before forming a line again to walk their way back home. Slowly, sloppy and in pain. Their bodies were aching and beaten, but nobody resisted. They all knew they wouldn't make it outside the home in the dust ocean. So they worked. Silently and in pain. They were all slaves by choice. And Jade hated it.

The sun danced on her face while she slowly lifted her heavy eyelids. How was that possible? They always went to work before sunrise. She lifted her aching body and looked through the window. The line of people were already walking towards the farm.

„Bastard." She said to herself while quickly dressing up and running downstairs. She knew Cain didn't wake her up on purpose. He loved to see her being beaten up. She rushed to put on her mask and grab her check-in ticket. Luckily, some people were still at the door. Including Dust. She stood in line behind him but neither of them dared to say a word.

CHAPTER 3

Viva la Resistance

CHAPTER 3: Viva la Resistance

She groaned in agony as the leather whip hit her back. She had enough. Enough of the oil farm, enough of the stupid prison home. She had her sights set on escaping. But instead of freedom she just felt fists against her back. She screamed at the top of her lungs until her eyes shot open.

„It was just a dream." Said Dust standing in her doorway.

„A dream of reality." She sighed

„I'm sorry about your wound." He said and took a step closer. His grey eyes were shining in the dark room. An oversized shirt was hanging off his shoulders like an old rag. He got sicker every day. She sighed.

„Come sit with me." He sat down beside her on the bed.

„Your sca-" She cut him off.

„No. I want to know about your sickness." He looked down at the dusty wooden floor.

„Why."

„You know. I care about you." He scoffs in disbelief. She was a cold-blooded soldier, though wasn't her fault as she took the camp worse than the others did. Regardless, he was still curious why. Despite his disbelief, he spoke.

„It's getting better." He lied.

„I know it's not true. You don't have to tell me if it's uncomfortable for you." He sighed and continued.

„I'm running low on medicine. There is probably not much I can do about it anymore."

„Don't say that!" His words made her stomach twist. She cared. Even if she didn't want to admit it. She wished she could help Dust, but she had no means of doing so. And she couldn't bring herself to steal. No. Never again. She grabbed Dust's hand and looked at him. For the record he looked kind of cute. His dirty blonde hair was messy and falling on his forehead. His eyes had a special kind of spark in them, despite all the pain and the sickness. Her cheeks reddened and she quickly looked away at his hand. It was pale. She could feel his bones through his thin skin. It sent shivers down her spine.

She laid down on her bed and so did he. She tried not to think about the camp but the sound, the smell flooded memories back into her mind. A tear rolled from her eye, but she didn't want to look weak. Dust noticed her quivering and put his hand on her shoulder.

„I'm here if you need me." He said and took in every feeling he had for her. He felt her chest rising and falling as she breathed heavily. He felt her hair tickling his shoulders as they fell from hers. He felt her body shaking in pain from work, but her beauty took the forefront of his attention. He drifted off to sleep, for the first time in 30 days. A peaceful night of sleep, anyway. Though she wanted to stay strong out of pride, she couldn't bring herself to do it anymore. She felt loved and appreciated after such a long time. She couldn't stop her tears.

Morning came as fast as they both fell asleep. As usual, every member of the home dressed up and lined up for work. She didn't know what was off with the day, but it felt out of place. It felt worse than any day before. She felt the hot gasses burning away at her skin and the chains gripping her wrists. She felt every trickle of sweat running down her back; every muscle in her body aching. And she had enough of it. Her determination to get out fastened. There were cars parked outside and thought she could take one of them. She craved the taste of freedom, yet it's always been so far away. Like a fresh drop of water in her dry cracked mouth. She lost herself in dreaming about freedom until a supervisor pushed her head down at the black oil.

She snapped.
She bashed the man's head with the chains locked on her arms, and convenient enough he had the keys to them. Quickly unlocking herself, she yelled in a raspy voice all over the farm.

Wasteland

„Who's with me?" Behind her a deep voice replied.

„Who dares to be with her?" It was Cain. Nobody moved an inch.

„Nobody. You're alone." He grinned.

„That doesn't mean I'm weaker." She smiled back, Envy kicked his knee down, and he fell to the ground as a group of guards rushed in her direction. She managed to fend off the first few just fine, but was swiftly put a stop to her rampage. They knocked her down and tied her together.

„Fine." She said. „Kill me."

„Kill you?" Laughed Cain now standing in front of her. „No. You don't deserve to die. You're going back to camp."

Her head hung heavy as her guts knotted up in her stomach. She felt dizzy. Gasping for air, she managed to mumble.

„No. Please. You can't do this." Cain kicked the

gasping Jade to the side and yelled out to everyone.

„If any of you try to do anything stupid you'll face the same fate as her!" Nobody dared to look up as they took her away. She cried and screamed, but they loaded her in a truck and walked away leaving her tied up, alone. After a few minutes, the doors opened again and a familiar voice is heard It was Dust's. But strangely, he didn't resist.

„Dust why are you here." She asked quietly.

„I was causing trouble."

„Don't lie to me." She said and looked away.

„I didn't want you to go alone. I know how horrible the camp was for you." They looked at each other. She noticed a purple bruise on his left eye.

„What did they do to you?"

„Oh it's just a scratch. It doesn't hurt." He lied and she knew it, but couldn't gather the strength to press for an answer. She laid on the floor, thinking about her fate. She was going back to the camp. She wished she had died in that stupid oil farm. She wished she could stay there forever. She didn't want to go back to that hellhole. She didn't want to see Ijos again. She had sworn to avoid the place as if it was sacred. But it didn't matter now. There's no way to turn the clock back. The memories from Ijos overwhelmed her again. Shamefully, she muttered;

„Can you hold me?" She didn't need to ask twice. Dust was already on his knees kneeling beside her. He dragged her into his arms and put his chin on her head. He hated seeing her crying. It broke something inside his chest.

Wasteland

CHAPTER 4

An Old Enemy

CHAPTER 4: An Old Enemy

The large wooden sign hanging above the road was grinning to Jade, as the supervisors pushed her through the gate. She didn't resist. She didn't scream or cry. Her face was as blank as a piece of paper. Dust was being pushed behind her. He, on the other hand looked terrified. They both knew what was waiting for them, but their fates were different.

„I'm sorry." She said quietly over her shoulder while they took her on the other side from Dust. He didn't know why they dragged her away. Everyone there had the same room and everyone ate together. They kicked him in the sleeping room. It was late and people were going to sleep. He looked at their lifeless faces. They were in pain, tired, hopeless. He had been there too.

„Tomorrow all the newcomers will be welcomed by the leader." Said a supervisor and grinned at the confused people looking around.

It was Dust's first time at the camp. It was a life sentence to slavery. He felt dumb for going after Jade. They aren't together anyway. He knew it wasn't her first time at the camp, but he knew something was off. He looked around the room. There were brown blankets scattered on the wooden floor. People slept on them. There was about a 100 of them. They were all wearing long brown tunics to cover their red, dust covered bodies. They reeked of sweat and waste. He sighed and followed the group of other new members. An old man, a middle-aged woman, some strange men and a few other people. They were all rebels against the leader. They all grabbed one of the blankets stacked in the corner and found their spot in the large- stable like looking- building. Dust found a place far back and laid down to rest.

Loud stomping caught his attention. There were 4 large men walking across the room, locking all the newly arriving members in chains. Only then, he noticed, that everyone was locked up in heavy metal chains. Their legs and arms were sore from the hard structures. He grunted as his chains locked into place. The humid odour of sweat made them question how many people died wearing them. Nobody had ever told him about how horrible the camp actually was.

Guards yelled everyone awake before sunrise. Dust didn't sleep well that night. In fact, he barely even slept. He wondered what happened to Envy. Guards led everyone to roll call. Heavy chains were chinking against each other to cover the screams and moans of their desperate souls. They stopped in front of a red coloured building. There was a staircase and a black figure was standing at the top. The leader spoke to them. In a loud, deep and chilling voice.

„It's your lucky day this month. I'm here to welcome all the new-comers who've arrived here in the past month."

The supervisors started pushing three fourths of the group forward. Including Dust.

„There are many of you." He paused. „Where are the others? For those of you who don't know already. They are dead."

Dust's stomach twisted. That means the majority of people working here die within a month. He wasn't going to be one of them. He was stronger than he looked. His chains clanged as the supervisors pushed the group ahead towards the factory. They will produce radioactive elements. A strong wind blew in their faces and suddenly they were standing in the middle of a huge dust cloud. Everyone started coughing and choking. Only then, Dust realised. They had no masks. Only the supervisors had them, while they were expected to fair without them. Dust sighed as they passed the cloud by. He hadn't seen Envy anywhere. Perhaps they killed her. He winced at the thought of it. No. That couldn't have happened. He lifted his head as they walked towards the large black chimneys rising their long necks towards the sky. The sky was still dark as they entered a long black hallway. They were now all dressed in the brown tunics and the cold stone ground was numbing Dust's bare feet. The sounds of heavy machines were filling the air. The people assorted themselves into three lines. The ones mining, people sorting and the rest working on the machines. Dust had to pick the mining. It was the order and the order was absolute. Each of them

Wasteland

were handed a large pickaxe and a flashlight to put on their head. They entered a long stone hallway and were greeted with the cold howling wind. At least there was no red dust down there. The sharp rocks dug into Dust's feet, giving him what felt like a million tiny cuts. He wanted to scream, but he shut his lip and visibly gulped his agony down. He took a few sharp breaths and lifted his chin. The supervisors arranged them into a straight line and yelled to start working. Dust began to swing his heavy tool toward the stone wall. It wasn't fair. They had machines for that kind of work so their efforts were practically useless. Dust sighed and took another swing at the wall. A few rocks flew in the air. An older woman, no older than 65 were mining next to him. The frail woman couldn't continue, so she leaned on the wall and took a rest. The supervisors came yelling at her and one of them tased her with God knows how many volts. She screamed and collapsed.

„She gone?" Laughed a guy that just came to check on them.

„Yeah. Nobody liked the old goat anyway." Grinned the other as they dragged her away. Dust clenched his fist, but continued mining.

Jade wasn't that surprised though. She knew the camp as well as every inch of it. No. it wasn't different from a year ago. Her face remained blank as they pushed her through the large metal gates. It remained blank when they pushed her to the ground. Her cheek hit the cold marble ground. Heat ran through her body and her eyes welled with tears. She peeled her cheek off the cold floor and looked up.

„Did you really think you won't come back here?" Laughed the dark figure sitting far back in the shadow. She knew him well. Too well in fact.

„Osen." She gritted her teeth.

„I see you still know me." He stepped from the shadow.

„Bow to the dark lord!" He yelled at her. She squinted at him. He was dressed in black and red. A long dark silk cape was flowing behind him with every step he took. His matte black chest plate was sleekly covering his shoulders. His metal gauntlets were reaching up to his elbows. He was wearing steel boots that made the floor howl every time he took a step. His clean marching echoed through the long room, as he was getting closer. She could now see his black eyes and brown hair. He looked beautiful but somewhat intimidating. He looked like the embodiment of power and fear. The cold-blooded killer.

„I said BOW to the dark lord!“ He repeated. This time he was standing only a few feet from the kneeling Jade. She was wearing heavy chains that were pushing her towards the ground, but she didn't bend. Not in front of him.

“I see you fancied up.” She said sarcastically.

„You're nothing but scum.“ He said and grinned at Jade. She couldn't bare the fact she had to bow before someone like him.

He was scum, not her. She was powerful, like she could be rid of hi with a snap of a finger if she so wished.

„That's not a good way to greet an old friend.“

„You're not my friend. Stop this madness.“ She talked back.

„Madness?“ He laughed „No. You got it all wrong. This is best for everyone in this world. I saved all of you ungrateful bastards.“ He looked at her dead in the eye.

„Get her out of the room.“ He gestured the supervisors to her..

They locked her behind metal bars in an isolated room. She too was handed an old dirtied blanket to sleep on. It was cold. Shivering, she layed in the cold of the night. It brought back every feeling from last year. How she worked all day. How she only got food and water once a day, the bare minimum to keep working away. The sounds of dying people. She was back. She thought that her escape would mean forever. She was truly going to die this time. There was no turning back. She wished to be back in Sehn in the home. But that was impossible now. Nobody could escape the large walls of Ijos anymore.

The blinding sun burnt her eyes when they were taking her across the burning hot ground towards the meeting hall. She looked rather humiliated. Her skin and hair were covered in red dust even if it was just the 3rd day at camp. Instead of taking the usual route towards the spinning wheel, they took her towards a large marble building. It looked beautiful. Like a castle. The large staircase lead up to the main door. It was made from stained glass in a variety of colours. It played with the light of sun rays, casting a rainbow all over the long hallway stretching in front of them. She knew where she was. It was Osen's mansion. But why would they take her there? They knew she was dangerous. They entered a large room including a throne and a smaller one on the other side. In the big one was sitting the so called- dark lord.

„Welcome my dearest Jade." He laughed.

„What do you want from me?" She hissed back at him.

„Perhaps you would have interest in my deal." A grim grin smeared across his face.

„I would never deal with you."

„Even for freedom?" He raised his eyebrows. Her body trembled at the word. She wouldn't make it at the camp. She knew that. She could see herself climbing a tall mountain, breathing in clean air. She could feel splashing of water beneath her feet. She could see the green grass growing on the hills.

„I'm listening." Was all she said.

„Very well." He said and snapped his thin fingers. »My offer is simple. Become my property- as a wife I mean and live well for the rest of your life." She gagged at the thought of it, but he wasn't done yet. „Or join my army in the north." His grin only got wider this time. No, she wouldn't do it. She wouldn't become one of his lady servants. She was better than this.

„Well?" He asked expectantly.

Her thoughts stopped on Dust. She had to take him with her. She couldn´t just leave him here.

„Where do I get my war outfit?" She sighed. She was going to war. She had to kill innocent people. But it was far better than becoming Osen's play doll.

A large grin cut through his face when suddenly the door shut open. A couple of supervisors shoved a person in front of Osen. She knew who it was. She almost yelled for him, but held back.

„Charon, young brother. We meet again at last." Osen hissed through his teeth.

„Do not call me by my name. You know I hate it. Blood was spilled over it. And more importantly don't call me your brother!" Yelled Dust. His voice was trembling. He looked terrible. Scars were covering his thin arms and his body looked weaker than ever.

„Don't play in front of the lady, young man. Remember why I sent you to Sehn. You failed not only I, but my empire. The lady changed your heart." he glanced over to Jade. „You are no longer welcome here brother." he said and signed the supervisors to take him away.

„Wait! What will you do to him?" She demanded.

„He will die outside. The disease is eating him alive anyway."

„Jade I'm sorry." He said quietly pulling his body closer to her. „I'm sorry I never told you about my step brother. I'm sorry I didn't take care of you better. I'm sorry we never found the mountain." He cried and his hand shook as he slowly wiped a tear from her cheek. She held his hand and screamed as the supervisors pulled her away and took him away.

„Such a pity to waste him like that." Laughed Osen and left the room slamming the door behind him. She listened to his steel boots clunking against the floor in the hallways behind the door. She collapsed on the floor and bawled. Charon wasn't a part of this family. He had told her that he was adopted. However, never talked about his family. She didn't care. She cared for him. He was a good person. And now he was gone...

Wasteland

CHAPTER 5

Fellow Warriors

CHAPTER 5: Fellow Warriors

The thought of having to kill for the dark lord turned her stomach around. She gagged as the supervisors took her to her cell. Nobody could explain the rage she felt. Her head was hot and her nails were jagged into her palms. She wanted to scream, but remained silent. Nobody could see her fury under her blank face. She looked somewhat sad but mainly careless. She couldn't even begin to imagine what will happen to Dust out there in the wasteland. No. She couldn't think about that. She couldn't think about his soft fingers wrapping around her waist. She couldn't think about his weak hand giving her strong support as they climbed endless mountains of despair. No. It was all gone now. But at the same time she was angry at him. Angry at him for not telling her the truth. Angry, because he knew the name of Osen Wisgard. The name every land from Ixah to Orbir trembled before. The name causing pain and destruction to every nation that ever existed. She loathed the name, and by proxy the whole family. They were the cause behind the endless war raging across the land. She clenched her fist at the thought of it.

But Dust was different. He hated the war. He didn't want destruction, pain or harm for anyone. Jade was almost sure he wouldn't hurt a fly if they still existed. He didn't fit into the puzzle. She sighed.

„Maybe it was all just a cover up." But it couldn't have been. No, the Wisgards were too proud to ever touch a peasant like her. But Dust wasn't like that. What did it matter now? He was gone. She had betrayed him. She didn't deserve to call herself his friend.

The cold floor sent a chill down her spine. It made her tremble on the thin blanket in the corner of a dark cell. It was autumn. She wished she had seen the colourful leaves before they were all burned to the ground. She imagined a cold breeze on her cheek, the red, yellow and orange leaves elegantly falling down from old wooden structures growing tall above her head. She imagined snowflakes, casting an icy wonderland over the fields, silently laying on the ground. It was beautiful. She imagined a blue sky and white clouds. They were fluffy like cotton candy. She thought of the bright yellow sun dancing with buildings of all colours. Green, blue, yellow, white and brown all clashed into a mixed rainbow of emotion. A slight grin appeared on her exhausted face. As she opened her eyes, she wanted to see all of it. But for that it was probably too late. She sighed and closed her eyes. A long day was waiting for her.

They woke up early in the morning.

„Get up!" Shouted someone in a familiar tone. He entered the cell. It was Cain.

„What are YOU doing here?" She smirked.

„I'm your general. Get up." His voice was cold and monotone. She quietly stood and walked behind him looking at her feet. They stopped in front of a large hall.

„Don't dare to try anything stupid." He hissed in her face close enough for her to feel his warm breath on her cheek. The odor of alcohol attacked her nose. Did this man never wash his damn teeth? She nodded and they moved inside. The hall was full of weapons and army uniform. Cain led her straight to one of the racks full of uniform.

„Change." He demanded.

„Could you turn-"

„I said change!" He shouted at her face. She turned around and quickly pulled off her clothes. It was humiliating for her. It felt like forever. She felt his eyes pierce through her scarred running body, cuts along her shoulder to her elbow, grinning at her. But she shamefully pulled on a black tunic and light pants in the same colour. The chest plate fit her perfectly. It was sleek and silver. It looked strong enough to stop a cannon ball. The shoes were made in the same style. Silver, tight boots made from steel. They were surprisingly comfortable. She took a gas mask from the rack and turned to face Cain.

„You look ridiculous. Women aren't good fighters." He smirked. If he knew, what she was capable of he wouldn't laugh at her like that. She clenched her jaw and let out a sigh. She didn't speak

Wasteland

though.

Her face was drained completely by the time they sat her down in the meeting room. She was sitting behind a table with 3 other people. They were all men, 2 of them were large. A mountain of muscles. The other one was had a rather normal build.

„Welcome the great warriors." Said Osen with a subtle voice. She took a good look of him. He was still wearing black with a long cape on his back. He looked rather young. He couldn't have been over 25.

„The powerful Warriors of the lands. Trained killing machines. Swift, strong steady and stealthy. An intimidating combination indeed." he laughed as one of the men growled.

„What a shame for us to treat the fine warriors with such disrespect." He continued in a belittling

manner. Jade quietly clenched her teeth.

„As you all recall. You took my offer. Including Jade." He glanced at her. „Which is surprising after she was offered a spot on my bed." He laughed. Her brows furrowed, but then remembered why she was here; She could be free, she could escape. It was her chance. She would rather die than be stuck in this rotting place.

„All of you will be deported to a 2 week training in Pourver." Continued Osen. „Then you will be transmitted in my base in Ixah You will protect it and attack Midgard from there. Sparrowtown is defeated already." He smirked at all 4 warriors.

„Your pathetic lives will finally be put at use." The warriors looked at each other with frowning faces. Jade couldn't deny the sorrow in her eyes. Nevertheless, it was either that or Ijos. They knew it all too well to stay there.

She sighed and looked through the metal of the ship. They were sailing down the river towards Pourver. The trip will take days. She wished they would at least lock them up together instead of separated. But it was clear everyone was scared of her. She was from Orbir. From Eidhen. She had spent her life training to become the great warrior of Orbir. She was trained to kill.

CHAPTER 5: Fellow Warriors

Wasteland

CHAPTER 6

Focus on The Training

CHAPTER 6: Focus on The Training

They showed them out of the ship like animals. With large chains on their legs and their hands tied on the back. Though relieved she was far far away from Osen, Jade was petrified. She had never been in the army before. Every mission she went on she was alone. She didn't need anyone. She was alone and she did well alone. No. She didn't need an army. She didn't need the stupid boot camp. She just needed to get in shape and gain some weight. She looked painfully thin. Everyone stared when they pushed the warriors trough a large corridor.

„I'll take Jade with me." Cain spoke from her left. She darted around and searched for the -so called- general. He was tall. Taller than usually.

„Welcome to Vormir." He grinned, flashing his yellow teeth. It made her want to vomit on the place, but she held back. Even when he grabbed her tied hands and pushed her in front of him into a dark corridor. She grunted as he gripped her neck and pushed her on a stage in front of - what looked like- hundreds of soldiers. There was dead silence in the large hall. They brought other 3 warriors as well. Cain started to shout.

„Welcome the most dangerous people in the world!" His voice was deep and raspy. „Murderers! Traitors!" Jade's rage was rising as he was shouting. „Welcome Dowak's warriors." Supervisors pushed the 2 large men on the stage and Cain continued.

„Strength." They quickly led them away.

„Ixah's warrior! Stealth." The procedure was repeated. And at last Cain called her out.

„Orbir's warrior." He made a pause „Trained by Arvas." A quiet hush began in the room after the supervisors took her away. They were all sceptical about letting her in the army. Damn right she was trained by Arvas. By the master of stealth. Master of all weapons.

And it wasn't easy being his student. Trained to kill wasn't a pretty fate. But what could she do. She didn't have parents anyway. It was the easiest place to survive.

But right now she didn't have time to think of the past. She had to focus on a plan to escape. She needed to get out of there as soon as possible. She sat down on a wooden table standing in the corner of her cell. Cain was standing in front of her.

„Tomorrow you will start with your two week training. I will be your guide. You will do as I say. Is that clear?"

„Yes." She sighed.

„Yes sir!" He pierced his raging eyes towards her.

„Yes sir." She repeated quietly. He quickly left the room and she was alone again. She didn't know what to expect from her training or the battle. The only thing she knew was that it won't be easy. But she was used to that. She never had it easy, yet she was here alive, brave and standing tall. After all, she was strong. Red moonlight replaced the burning hot sun filling her room. It was calm and peaceful. Almost pretty. She couldn't sleep. Her mind kept jumping from war to freedom. To green grass, to lime trees and blue sky. Yes. It was the most beautiful thing she could ever have imagined. She had enough of red, enough of dust and dry air that reeked of poisonous gas.

CHAPTER 7

The Taste of Freedom

CHAPTER 7: The Taste of Freedom

The sun flashed through the broken glass on the floor. It was easier than she had expected. They had been fools to let them train like this and Jade thought they would have known better. She grinned. slipping through the small opening and ran towards the wall as the guards were running after her. Anyone who tried to stop her met their death immediately. Osen severely underestimated her. A week of training was enough for her to regain all her strength. She lunged onto the tall wall. Glancing back at the top. Cain was standing there, with a smile printed on her face. He saw her looking at him and nodded. It almost seemed like he was training her for something he couldn't do himself; to escape... Her feet hit the ground on the other side of the wall. She was outside, and thus free. She didn't have to do more practise, and stronger by the week. Prepared, she ran and ran until she reached a meadow. She was far far away from the camp now. She didn't have to kill for Osen. And the army won't notify him of her escape. Otherwise he would have dealt a cruel at death to them all. She grinned a wistful smile at the mere thought of freedom. The yellow muddy grass, has slowly transformed into a lush green field. She hadn't seen grass this natural-looking in so long. As she walked on, small bushes had poked at her attention. They grew into larger ones, some even into trees. Jade couldn't believe her eyes; there were still trees in Ixah. Her heart jumped as she touched the leaves. She heard the wind humming in the leaves and grass. It was beautiful.

She didn't remember much of Ixah. After all, she spent most of her time training with Arvas. Orbir wasn't suitable for training, so they moved her to Ixah when she was 5 years old. She lived there until her young adolescence. At 15 years old, Ixah was attacked. Fortunately enough, she had finished the training by then. Somehow, the army invaded their base at night and most were eliminated on the spot, others left alive to serve Osen. He was 17 at the time. His father died and left him the throne at such a young age. Jade was put into a working camp where they forged weapons for the royal army however, the rebel she was, she kept causing trouble. Especially one time where she had crossed the line. She slaughtered a supervisor in cold blood during her desperate attempt to escape. That secured her a spot in Ijos, at the mining slave camp. Where people wore chains, torturously whipped and treated like scum. She didn't know why, but a year and a half later they put her in the home in Sehn. She was surprised that she survived a year and a half in Ijos. Even the ones with the higher chance of survival only held up for no longer than 9 months. They didn't have any masks there, therefore lung infections and such became the norm. She clenched her fist at the sudden realisation she was back in Ixah she knew all too well.

Although she lived here, she never saw the joyous side of it. People always seemed gloomy and quiet. They seemed drained and tired, but she sighed and walked on. She was near Sparrowtown; the stone city. It was grey and sad. The streets were empty and it looked like a ghost town, not a single entity in sight. It made her skin crawl at times. Fast wind was howling around the corners of the streets and houses. Dark puddles of waste were tainting the pathways, making it hard to walk. However, she didn't need a mask as the shores of Ixah were still free of the dust. The purity and beauty of nature placed a sweet smile on her face. Too bad people were mislead to an ocean of dust in their lives. She smirked and kept walking. The colourful roofs were scattered all over the place. It looked like a rainbow spilled on the street and left a mark.

She regretted not being able to see the three cities more often. In fact, she never saw Virigor. It was the richest part of Ixah. People said that it was full of bliss. It was said that the buildings were covered with pearls and crystals. That the roofs were made of stained glass and smooth marble. Only the prestigious could afford to live there, but she was desperate to see it. She wanted to dress in a beautiful grown and dance away the night under the glass roof and a diamond chandelier. Jade sighed. What was the use of dreaming about something that was gone and out of reach? She remembered Dust and how she just left him there to die. She was heartless to the core. Anger filled up her body and she clenched her fist in response. Life wasn't fair. She just wanted to be happy. She wanted

Wasteland

to live free and- Oh well. It was what it was. She had to be happy with it. She had no other chance. At least she was free from the pain in Ijos. She could do anything she wanted now. She was her own queen.

After a few weeks, she arrived in Mitgard. Although some people still lived there, It was torn down for the most part. However, it was good enough to find some food and shelter at the very least. She searched the market for any scrap of something to eat. She found a few pieces of old bread and a few apples.

„It'll do." She shrugged and stored away.

She ran across the street and disappeared into the alley.

CHAPTER 8

Finding a Purpose

CHAPTER 8: Finding a Purpose

She often heard stories about what Ixah used to look like before, but it was hard to believe them. Not with the way it was then. War, tears, destruction and loss were all common things to experience. They say Vigrior used to be bright and shiny, that Midgard was alive and happy. However, she couldn't believe it. There was no way. They all knew we would eventually fall. No great city could survive anymore. Borderlands were destroyed years ago and nobody knew the name of the underground mega city anymore. Like they never even existed. Entire races were being wiped out of existence. this was the world she knew... the war started on the year she was born.... she didn't have her parents anymore... She wished she could say that they died for her to survive, or that they died fighting for the city. but honestly she had no idea where they were or what happened to them. They left her on the street to die when she was 5 years old. She didn't even care anymore and if she learned, anything in the 18 years of her life was that you can't trust anyone. People are cold, careless and full of hatred. And she knew she wasn't any better. She had never been a good person. She's done heinous things like stealing all the money from a homeless man when she was 10 for food. she lost her only friend when she was 12. By the age of 14, she stopped talking to people. and she killed, hardly ever for the right reason. A week ago she compulsively stabbed a man in the chest and she didn't know why. She just wanted to get some money and clothing. But her motive was still unclear to her. She didn't know the man but she was so mad.

It was late at night. As usual, she couldn't sleep so she was sitting on the ground and looking at her silver blue knife shining in the moonlight and there was this man. He looked like a regular citizen of Midgard, nothing really stood out from his appearance. The middle layer in society. He was holding a suitcase. Of course, she could just grab his suitcase and run. But she didn't have the power to. So she quietly stood up and hid behind a wall. As the man walked by the knife silently flew to his back. He let out a small cry and fell to his knees. He just barely broke his fall with his arms. When she saw what she had done her blood ran cold. Her palms become sweaty and she just stood there, watching the poor man lay alone on the cold dark street. But she wasn't sad, nor did she feel regret. She was just shocked how horrible of a person she was. She stood there in the dark for a long time. Picking up his warm coat, she put the knife behind her belt. Without any further thought, she grabbed the suitcase and scurried. She ran as fast and as far as she could. The cool air was blowing against her cheeks. The sturdy concrete was helping her launch herself forward. she took a large step and pushed herself up a wall. Grabbing the ledge, she managed to pull herself up. The wall was broken down and tons of tiny pebbles dug into her palms as she pushed herself up. Not minding the pain, she ran along the narrow top of the wall and climbed up to the roofs. Midgard had its roofs close together and connected. She could easily jump from one to the other. She ran for a bit and stopped on a blue and white roof. She had her shelter there. It was just a cloth placed over a broken roof in an attempt to patch it. She moved the cloth away, giving her access down. The wooden floor creaked under her weight as if it was about to break. She looked around the tiny attic. There was a torn mattress in the corner of the room. A dirty pillow was lying on it and half of a blanket was awkwardly placed on the floor. In the other corner, there was a chair in front of a broken piece of a large mirror she was using to see herself in. She collapsed on the mattress and threw the suitcase on the floor. She was so alone. She had nobody to care about, nobody to talk to. A small tear ran down her cheek. She closed her eyes and weeped. She missed Charon so very much.

The next day she woke up to the sound of shots being fired on the street. She could hear people screaming. They broke into Midgard. Jade thought quick and launched herself up to the roof. She turned her head to the right and saw some soldiers marching into the street. It was Osen´s army. The emotionless beings without any feelings or empathy or mercy. Nobody ever succeeded defending the city from them. They cast terror everywhere they set foot on..

Her thoughts returned to reality. People said that Midgard was safe and well protected but as usual, people were wrong. She peeked from behind a wall. The sky was cloudy and dark, but no airships could be seen hovering on it. She jumped down and looked around the street. There was a little boy and his mom. He was holding her hand and they were both running down the street. The little guy was about 4 years old. It seemed like his little legs couldn´t keep up with his mom. They separated, but the mom didn´t care. She just kept running. The boy tripped and fell down. He sat up and started crying for his mom

"Mother you forgot me!"

She didn´t turn around and disappeared behind a building. She just left him....

Jade´s mind went silent. All the shots, all the screams faded away in the background. Her thoughts were focused on the boy. His crying became louder and louder. It flashed back her memories from when she was left on the street. She remembered her mom pushing her away to the ground and walking away. She ran after them but she just yelled back at her.

"You have to leave me alone! You must be alone! Leave us alone!"

She didn´t understand. That was her family. She belonged to them. She was sure they just went to the shop and they would be back in an hour. So she sat there...on the ground. She sat for an hour; a few hours...they probably stopped for a coffee. She sat for a day... there was an accident on the road. She was sure they would come back soon. So she sat. For a week, a month. She sat for a year! And sometimes she still did. She sat on the ground waiting for someone to love her.

She snapped back to the real world again and in the little boy, she saw herself. The girl who was waiting for someone to save her. She couldn´t let this happen to him. She held back for a moment and the army marched into the street. Without thinking, she launched herself down the road. And grabbed the kid. She hugged him tightly and ran as fast as she could down the street into the Labyrinth of houses. She carried him into her shelter and sat down on the mattress. He was scared to death. His eyes were red from crying and his nose was stuffy. She looked at him closely. He was small and weak like he hasn't eaten in weeks. Without thinking she walked over to her mostly empty food storage. She opened the heavy lid and it made a loud creaking noise. She grabbed a piece of bread. The biggest one out of the four she had in total. Looking at the shameful condition of the meal, she decided to take some cheese from her secret storage. She took a glass of water for herself and sat next to the little boy on the chair. She realized she didn´t even know who he is.

"So what's your name? " She asked carefully.

"North. " He replied, munching down his bread.

She tried to seem cheerful. "Where are you from kiddo? "

"I'm from the Sparrowtown."

"Oh really? Me too! " She lied.

He looked at her with big frightened eyes. "Are you nice? "

"of course! I'll take good care of you. " She smiled.

"But I have my mom. "

The words stopped in her throat.

 "Right? " He asked carefully.

"Sweetie your mom isn't coming back. " She tried her best not to sound so hopeless.

"Why? Doesn't she love me? "

"she does.... But..."

"but what? " His eyes filled with tears.

"She wanted to keep you safe and said I could take care of you. " She quickly made up the lie.

"oh... Well okay... But who are you? "

"My name Is Jade. " She smiled to him.

She was in shock. She just said she´s going to take care of a kid. She couldn't do that. She couldn't give him enough love... But he was just so cute. She couldn´t waste a life like that. She could manage just fine. She had to do this! She slowly stood up and looked through the window. There was black smoke all around the city, smearing soot onto the buildings and ground. Then she looked back at North. He was happily munching away at his sandwich and swinging his leg back and forward on the chair. For the first time she took a good look at him. He had blond hair, almost white. Only one strand of his hair was dark brown. It seemed special. Her eyes stopped on his tiny stuffed cheeks. They were a little blushed and chubby. His nose was small and lifted a bit upwards to his eyes. He had a deep dark blue shade of eyes. They seemed like endless deep oceans pierced with little silver stars shining within them. The lips were rather small and a pink brown colour. He was quite small. An oversized white shirt was hanging from his shoulders, held up with a rope belt. He had some brown pants on his legs and winter boots on his feet. The boots reminded her. Winter was just around the corner!

CHAPTER 9

Living on The Edge

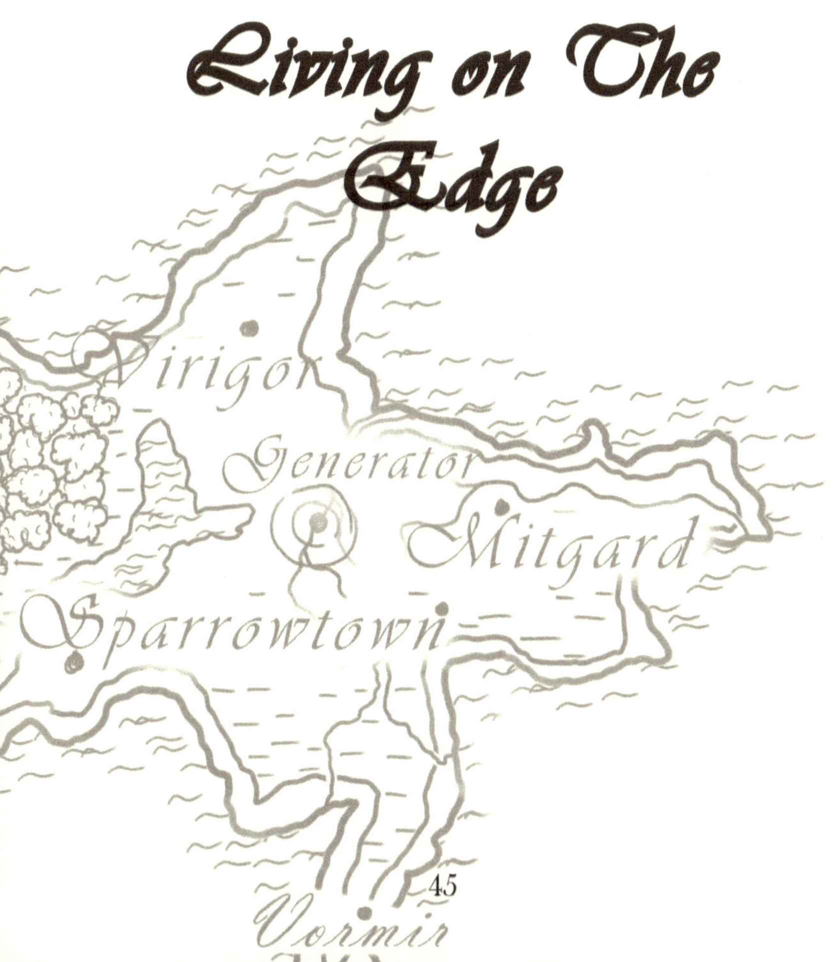

Wasteland
CHAPTER 9: Living on The Edge

So the winter passed by. They had a full chest of food. Jade mostly got it from stealing, but she didn't mind anymore. North was doing well and it seemed like he was starting to trust her. They would often sit on the mattress and talk or draw on the floor. For the first time in a long time, she was finally having some fun and she really felt like she had someone she can care about. She felt like she had a brother and she took good care of him. He told her stories of his family every day.

"I have three sisters. We used to live in a very big house in Sparrowtown. Our room was round with 4 beds. We each had a name that matched our position in the room. West, South, East, and me. Well one day a soldier came into our city at night. When I woke up everyone was gone and mom was crying. She said they went on vacation but they never came back. Neither did we. I left the house with mom and we came here."

"Wow it seems like you had fun with your sisters." exclaimed Jade.

"Not really. They didn't like me very much." the young boy replied.

"Oh. Why not? "

"Well I guess I was different. They look the same but I didn't look like them at all. "

"Maybe he's adopted" she thought to herself. But she never payed it too much thought. She did notice how smart he was though. He seemed almost magical too. He could be one of those hybrids maybe. No. She was crazy. Or maybe not. There were rumors, that somewhere outside of this world, beings were divided into groups such as demons, elves, some fairies should still be alive and many more. And there were normal people like Jade. Beings should never mix with other species as the risk was extremely dangerous. But like the Romantic Romeo and Juliet some of them fell in love. And a few so-called hybrids managed to survive. They said only three were found and brutally killed. As she watched North she noticed a few odd things about him. Like his extremely white hair with a dark lock on the left side of his head. He had incredibly pale skin and his ears were a bit pointy. But there's no way. They say that elves distanced themselves from the war at its very beginning and have been locked away ever since. She quickly shook that thought off. It was beginning to get warmer outside. And they were both starving. They had just stolen some apples and grapes from the market and now they were back at her shelter.

North was munching on a chocolate bar Jade gave him a few minutes ago. She sat down in front of the glass in her room. She had changed so much since she was a kid. Her hair used to be short and cut uneven. She had chubby cheeks and freckles, even though she still had them. Her hair was light brown she always put it in a braid so it didn´t get in the way of her work. While looking at herself she noticed a dark box in the corner of the glass. She looked under the table where the dark thing was placed and re-membered. It was the suitcase she took from the poor man she killed back then. Before not having opened it, she pulled it out. It had a lock system. She could go on trying to guess the code, but time was scarce. She took a small axe she found on the floor once and smashed it on the suitcase. Once, twice, again, and suddenly it opened. She ripped it open with excitement. She felt like a little kid on Christmas morning.

On the inside, she found a computer storage device. Like a USB but it could store much larger files. People stole them from Osen´s army and called them plugins. There were about 10 such plugins reported. Now of course! The problem was she didn´t have a computer. And she couldn't just steal one. They were very hard to get since the war had started. She put the plugin away and dug into the files that were printed out and put in the case. »the tree of ru-ins« the title caught her attention immediately. She had read about this. The tree of ruins was a tree all legends about hybrids talked about. The legend said that this massive tree protects the souls of every magical being in the world. It said that's the one who climbs it and enters the secret portal will get the chance to see the souls of each and every magical being that ever lived. Every new Leaf that appeared was a new soul. The leaves that fall down are beings who died already. But the leaves on the ground could transform into roots of the empire. Although it sounded enchanting, it was just a legend. And legends like that never turn out to be true. It just seemed stupid. Like yeah her grandpa supposedly turned into the root. She shook her head and unfolded the papers. They excited her because they might give her some answers about the old tree. But to her disappointment it was just some information about handling the plugin. She was rather disappointed. She was hoping for some epic reveal of the meaning of life but without a computer, her hands were tied together.

Jade threw the papers on the ground and laid down on the mattress. North was looking at her very confused.

"What's wrong?" he asked.

"Ugh! I need a computer"

"Well we had a laptop back in our apartment." She jumped on her feet.

"Pack your stuff! " She exclaimed.

"Why, what's wrong?"

She smiled at him slightly. "We're going to Sparrowtown!"

 They grabbed a few apples and some bread then they set off to Sparrowtown. It was the poorest part of Ixah. But by poor she didn´t mean in the way of poverty. They had everything. It just wasn't as glamorous as Vigrior. North and Jade stepped out onto the street and ran along the grey dirty houses. Midgard had really changed for the worst since the army broke in.

"Be careful little buddy. Hold onto me and don't get yourself lost please." She said to North. She was scared to death but she couldn't show it to him. He needed to feel protected.

"Sure thing Jade." They sneaked into the outer ring of the city. There was a huge wall there. She took a step under it and looked up. It was about 10 meters high. Without thinking, she leapt up and started climbing. When she reached the top she heard soft voice

"Jade you forgot about me! I can't climb!"

"Oh my God I'm so sorry North!" she immediately felt bad.

"It's okay just help me up." He smiled.

"Um North I need you to climb and reach for my hand okay!? "

"Okay." He pushed his tiny hand forward and grabbed a rock sticking out of the wall. He was doing well, pushing forward his little light body. He stepped on the last rock high enough for him to reach for her hand. And to her horror the rock slipped out of wall. North was left hanging from the wall holding on to it with his hands.

"North! Are you okay? "She shouted down at him.

"Yes I am but I can't hold on much longer." His hand was shaking-ly gripping the wall.

Just then, when she thought things couldn't get any worse soldiers marched into the alley. The terror paralyzed her whole body. After a few short moments, North´s voice dragged her out of her trance.

"Jade you have to go without me." His voice was shaking.

"No! I will not leave you like this! "

"But you will die. I don't want you to die." His words remained firm in her head. Someone cared about her the same way she did. He would die for her. She didn't care if it was just a little boy she didn't want to lose the one she promised to protect!

"Jade I can't hold on anymore. "

She quickly let down her leg. "Okay North I need you to let go of the wall and grab my leg."

He let go of the wall and his other hand slipped a little. Her heart was racing and her hands were shaking, shutting her eyes in desper-ation to not watch him die. Suddenly, she felt his tiny arms on her leg. She tried to pull him up but her shoe slipped. North fell down the wall as she shot herself behind him and grabbed his hand.

"I got you!" She pulled him up and laid down on the top of the wall and they both panted loud and quick. She looked up and smiled at him.

"Good job, little guy." He gave her an indescribably thankful look.

They continued the path with no bigger issues other than just some soldiers and people on the streets. Sparrowtown used to be the bus-

Wasteland

iest part of Ixah. Now the streets were mostly empty and deserted. The whole Sparrowtown had been mined into rock centuries ago. There were two parts to it. In the back and the close. They were connected with a hanging bridge. It looked absolutely beautiful. They were walking along an alley when suddenly North tugged on her shirt.

"I know where we are! "

"Okay kiddo lead the way." He ran off.

"Whoa... Slow down a bit!" She ran after him into the streets, across some bridges, under the rocks until they stopped on a small square.

"Why did you run so fast?" She turned around and saw North walking behind her. She shook her head and looked at him with wide eyes.

He just shrugged. "Let's just go in," he said.

The house was green. It was rather tall and narrow. She put her hand on the wooden door. It rustled a bit but wouldn't open. The iron has served its due and needed to be replaced. She stepped a few steps back and lunged into the door. She pushed her body against the hard door. They broke down with ease and she fell on the ground hitting her head on the glass. Blood ran down her forehead and she lost the sense of reality. Everything became foggy and dark. The last thing she could remember was north's tiny silent footsteps running across the rock floor.

Seemingly moments later, she woke up in a bed. It was soft and cosy. When she looked around the room, she noticed there was blood on the floor. That made her remember what happened. She stood up and walked over to a large mirror in the room. It was broken and black from some kind of smoke. What happened here? She thought to herself. It couldn't had been Osen. The door was closed! She looked in the mirror. There was blood all over the right side of her face. She moved her brown hair to reveal a large wound on the side of her head. She felt sick but had to find water. She couldn't afford an infection now. She opened the door of the room and found herself in a small corridor. When she looked to the right, she could see the bathroom. It was at the very end. She slowly started walking but with every step she took, Jade felt dizzier. Crawling along the hallway was almost the most humiliating thing she had ever done. Somehow, she made her way to the sink and picked herself up. There was a small drawer. She grabbed the handle and pulled. There was some pure alcohol in there. Even though she didn't want to do it she knew she had to. She reached for the alcohol, hands shaking from the excruciating pain. She turned around to catch a quick glimpse of the room. It was dimly lit from the light coming through a tiny window. Its furniture was made from white wood. There was a small table with cosmetic stuff on it. The walls were painted light brown. She slowly leant to the bottle and heard the alcohol pour out. A sharp burning pain ran through her body as it hit her skin. She writhed in agony and waited for the pain to end. She looked disgustingly at the wound in the mirror. Jade took one of the towels and wrapped it around her head. She stepped back to the hallway and called out for North. No answer. Where could he be? She opened all the doors slowly moving down the hallway and finally. There was a round room. It looked like a compass. She saw North tucked in a small bed beside the window. There were toys scattered around the floor. She gently shook North and he opened his eyes.

"Hey buddy. Good morning." He slowly lifted his little head up. At first, he didn´t recognise her at all.

"Oh! Hello Jade! "He was chipper as always, and was thrilled to show Jade all of his old toys. She didn't pay much attention, but she listened to him ramble anyways; he was just a kid after all. So she let him play and sat down beside him. While he was playing, she decided to take a quick look around the room. She noticed something weird in one of the beds. Her first guess was an animal seeking shelter. She took her knife out and slowly approached the thing lying in bed. She reached for the blanket and slowly pulled. The horrifying scene left her frozen in place. The decomposing corpse of a rotting child; hair had fallen out and her skin took on a sickly green shade. Hoards of maggots had invaded and made home of her lifeless body, squirming in and out of any opening they had. She couldn't even comprehend what she saw. Next arrived the smell, triggering a gag reflex. There was a little girl laying in the bed.

Wasteland

Her skin was pale, her hair was falling out and her eyes were wide open. Her green dress was soaked in blood. She almost screamed but held back. North didn't notice anything, so she quickly threw the blanket over the body and shouted

"North! We are leaving! "

"Can I take some toys with me?" He looked at her with hopeful eyes.

"Of course. Where was the laptop?" She said with a pale face.

He was still happy. "it's packed in your bag!"

"North, you are golden!" She managed to give him a small grin.

She just heard him let out a small giggle. She grabbed her backpack and North´s hand and ran outside. Out on the street she turned to North. This little buddy saved her dumb ass yesterday.

"Thank you kiddo." She said and stroked his white hair.

He didn´t say anything, but gave her a slight smile.

CHAPTER 10

Missed Opportunities

CHAPTER 10: Missed Opportunities

Their trip back to Midgard was quiet, peaceful and slow. Her head was still burning from the pain caused by the wound, but the important thing was that they arrived safely. She stepped to the chair and sat down. With a loud inhale she took off her backpack. It was green and rather large. It had many clips, pockets, and zippers. It was kind of army-esque but not the Osen kind. She liked it. The backpack rustled as she put it in her lap. The old zipper kept getting stuck as she pulled it. She took out the laptop. It was white with some grey, black and silver lines for decoration. It looked rather fancy and cool. Her palms were getting a bit cold on the steel so she rubbed them together and blew in them. She opened the laptop and pressed onto the power button. It made a quiet creaking sound and the light turned on. The screen lit up and a Crystal-like logo appeared. It was just when she got hyped and excited the screen went black. It stayed like that for a few seconds and then a red picture with low battery sign appeared.

"I should have known!" She screamed and slammed the laptop closed. North looked at her, confused.

"What's wrong?" He asked.

"The damn battery was empty"

"Well can't you just charge it?"

„I would, but I don't have a charger... or maybe I do!" She exclaimed. "Wait here North!" She jumped off the mattress and ran off into a place that used to be a library once. It had computers in it but they were all broken.

"I'm sure I'll find some cables that can be used." She said to herself. Jade stopped in front of the large building. The door was made of glass, and she started to panic. What if she hurts herself again? What if she gets another wound? She was scared to death but she had to do this. She couldn't give up now after getting so far. But she was so scared. Glass was horrible. It was awful! With difficulty, she set her fear aside and bravely took a step forward. She reached out her hand and prayed for the door to be unlocked. She would never be able to smash it as fear overcame her. Her palm held onto the wooden door knob and her fingers wrapped around it. She gently pulled at the door made a creepy loud sound. It was open!

She swung the door open and stepped in. The place was round and large. There were bookshelves all over the walls and the staircase was going up all the way to the top. There were different colourful books all over the place. Some were torn and destroyed laying on the floor. The sound of her footsteps echoed in the large room as she walked across to the computer corner. She just needed to get the hell out of this place as soon as possible. It creeped her out. She grabbed some cables and ran as fast as her body would let her. Adrenaline levels in her body were rising and she felt the power in her legs. She was still in good condition from the training in Vormir. She launched herself onto a balcony and up to the roof. She stopped there for a breather. The fresh air filled up her lungs. It got a lot warmer, and she walked slowly from then on. Since she met North she didn't really have time for herself. She enjoyed the sun on her cheeks. The heat was warming up her whole body. She looked up to the sky, met with greyish blue clouds, like someone painted on it. When she looked down she could see colourful roof-tops all over the place. On her right was a large building that was once used for meetings. It had golden window frames and a purple roof curved different shapes. The whole city looked like something out of a fairy tale. It had gotten a lot darker since the war. She didn´t want to go back yet, so she sat there in the sun with her body leaning back and her hands resting for support. It was warm and comfortable so she lied down and let her body rest. She felt the hot roof warming her up and her mind flew away. She thought about how the world used to be. She thought about her family, though it wasn't a sad memory. She let it go years back but they were a good memory after all. Her dad looked like her, resembling her brown hair and bright blue eyes. He was rather tall and had the most beautiful smile she had ever seen. Her mom was the complete opposite. She had light blonde hair and green eyes. Her face was blushed and covered in freckles. And she was their mix. She wished she turned out as beautiful as them. But she guessed that's up to luck and as far as she knew she had never been really lucky.

Opening her eyes, the once light grey had darkened. It was apparent that she fell asleep, leaving North alone. In a rush of regret, she made her way over to her shelter and looked around the room. She sighed at the sight of North sleeping on the mattress. The little guy was tired. She stroked his hair and started searching the cables. Finally, she found the right one, but she needed something to charge it from. She kept thinking what she should do. And eventually, she got an idea. Of course! How could it have been so obvious? She lived on top of a house, so itt must have had some electricity inside. The only problem was that it was full of acids and torn down. Well she had nothing left to do so she just hoped that they had disappeared by now. The access to the house was through the floor of the attic. A wooden trapdoor had to be lifted. She packed the laptop's cable as well as the weird looking drive, and pulled a rope tied to the trapdoor. It creaked and opened with a loud bang. There was a ladder under it.

She stepped on it carefully and started climbing. Every footstep sounded like the house was about to crumble and fall apart. Eventually, she made it. Slowly but surely. "It should become easier from now on!" She took a light step but to her surprise the floor beneath her opened and a big hole introduced itself. Her heart jumped and stops for a second. She managed to catch herself on a fence near the staircase. She let out a silent cry of terror. The fear made her eyes water and a tear dropped down the hole. It was about 3 floors deep. She slowly made her way across the staircase. The house seemed nice. It was rather large and had many rooms but they were all completely destroyed. She walked through the hallway and stopped in a room full of broken computers. Skimming and scanning throughout the room, she had found it. In the corner she could see cut through wires. She cut through her cable with a knife. She wished she could say she knew what she was doing. She just connected some wires and hoped for the best. She plugged the laptop in and to her fortune a green light appeared and the laptop started up. Luckily, there was no password. There was a few files on the desktop; in one there was music. She opened a song called "In The Mountains" and searched forward. There were some random images of North´s family. She kept scrolling down.

There were pictures of his mom and dad. His sisters as babies and growing up. But only one picture of North. She found it strange but ignored it. She took her backpack and pulled out the plugin. It was black and heavy and there was a little green tree on it. It fit perfectly! When she plugged it in, a loading screen appeared. But it required a password.

„Damn it!" She took the papers she found with the plugin. She noticed weird looking curved letters on them. Although they were ineligible, she hoped maybe North could derive meaning from them.

„North! Can you come down here?"

„Where?"

She realized she didn't tell him where she was going.

„Why is there a hole in the floor?" He yelled from the attic.

„Just climb down it." She could hear him step on the ladder and walk across to the staircase.

„Watch out for the hole." She yelled.

„Okay."

He walked into the room she was in. He looked scared.

„What was this place?"

„It's just a house, buddy. Calm down."

„It's scary"

„Don't Worry. Just come here. Can you read this?" She showed him the green sparkly letters.

„Of course! My dad taught me." Score! She thought to herself.

„What does it say?" She asked nervously.

„It says: "We are the ones to fight and survive. Soldiers of night.""

„Thank you so much little guy." She said trying to sound as calm as possible. She slowly typed in.

-- fight--

[Wrong]

--survive—

Wasteland

[Wrong]

--soldiers in the tree of ruins—

[CORRECT]

She made it.

The folder opened and there was a text file inside. It was large and all the letters were tiny. She started reading.

When she finished reading she leaned backwards.

„So that's it. An invitation."

North was asleep on her lap. There was no way she would leave him alone. The file was about the war. How they need more soldiers and something about the connection to the tree of ruins. It said the researchers found it was in some way connected to souls or more likely people. But it was all still a big mystery. It was an invitation to the war against... who? Her heart skipped a beat. Who was brave enough to stand up to Osen?

The other part of the file said „You have come to the point where your life changes. You have to know the importance of this. You cannot tell anyone about it. We are reaching out to you because you can help us. We know you can kill. You proved yourself. We ask you to join a mission that could end the 2 decades long war."

Her stomach turned around when she read about the killing. That poor guy did nothing to her. She shouldn't have killed him. Her mind was racing but she read forward.

„We cannot force you into collaboration or participation. We will not hurt you. We only ask for 2 things: You have to keep quiet about this and consider the following offer.

We are offering you a place in our rebellion. You will be sent to a mission. You probably know Osen and his army. We can't tell you what exactly your task is as we don't know yet. Keep in mind that with signing the contract we do not guarantee your safety and survival. We think you are prepared for this because of your killing, computer hacking and tactical skills. With signing the contract, you enter the elite rebellion system of Ixah. We will provide you food, clothes, medicine and a place to stay for the price of your life.

Useful information:

--mission starting on April 23 next year--

--all supplies are free--

--mission will last a maximum of 2 weeks--

--safety is not granted.--

If you choose to enter we ask you to search „apply" and give us some more information.

Thank you for your time"

„Neat." She almost shouted out. She could have free food as well as medicine, and she wouldn't be homeless if she was lucky enough to survive 2 weeks in the centre of war.

With a sad smile she slowly typed out „A P P L Y" a list of random missions appeared she searched for the one she read about and saw the [APPLY] button. She hovered the mouse over it but stopped. What about North? She promised to take care of him. And he needed her.

She sighed and slowly closed the tab and unplugged the computer. She lifted up the sleeping kid, grabbed her stuff and returned to the attic. She opened the laptop once again and searched the music file. She scrolled down looking for a song and almost laughed when she spotted the ironically titled song „new opportunities "she clicked it and a slow guitar tune started playing. She looked out the window and jumped to the roof. She leaned her back on it and watched the sun slowly set behind the rainbow of colourful city roofs. The wind was blowing in her face and playing with her hair. The calming guitar song was playing in her ears. She wished she could just leave her life behind and start a new one at this point. A better one.

CHAPTER 11

Shattered Trust

CHAPTER 11: Shattered Trust

A loud crashing sound teared apart the song. It came from the inside.

„North! Are you okay?"

„That wasn't me Jade!"

She launched herself inside and stuck her head in the hole in the floor. She could hear loud footsteps coming closer.

„That cannot be good. North run!"

She grabbed the backpack and quickly stuffed some food inside. She leaped across the roofs and looked around to find North. She saw him running over a bridge placed between 2 tall houses. The footsteps behind her were getting louder every moment. She forced herself to jump up the big wall in front of her. When she grabbed the top, her hand slipped on a piece of glass and cut her palm open. The pain was almost unbearable but she had to get over the wall somehow. She closed her eyes, forced her body up, and rolled to the other side. Forcing the scream down her throat, she clenched her palm.

She ran across the bridge and passed a few roofs before she turned around to see what was after her. The flesh hunters. They were kind of like mafia but worse. They looted and took down people's homes and sold the people to rich bastards. They were cold blooded and didn´t show any mercy to others. While she was busy looking backwards she didn't notice she got trapped. In front of her, there was a dead end and behind her were the hunters. She couldn´t run anymore. So this meant fight.

She wrapped her fingers around the knife hanging behind her belt and slowly turned around. She could now feel her blood from the wound running down her hand, but there was no time to focus on the pain. She looked around to find her enemy. She spotted them on her right. There were two men and a woman all dressed in black but had different colours of socks, gloves and masks. One man had green, the other blue and the woman was in red. Adrenaline ran through her body and her heart was trying to beat out of her chest. When they came closer, she noticed an ugly scar one of the men had on his face. The woman looked rather weak but extremely fast.

She pulled out her knife and put her hands in front of her. The knife shone in the sunlight right before dark clouds hovered on the sky. They got close and she could clearly see the evil grin on the large man´s face. He threw a small butterfly knife at her and it got stuck in the wall behind her back. She grabbed it and threw it back at him with all the force she had. Of course, she missed, but he didn´t know her plan. He just laughed in a horrible loud voice. At that moment, she took her silver knife and launched it forward. It felt like the world slowed down for a bit. She could hear her loud nervous breathing. The knife rotated twice in the air and then pierced into the man´s chest. It took him a moment to analyse the situation. He collapsed and screamed in agony. It was an ear-tearing scream of surprise and anger. She ran to him and kneeled down.

"Sorry..."

She quietly squeezed out of herself, grabbed the knives and looked up only to see the woman´s surprised face. She stood up and took a step forward. She could barely hold herself back from crying when she stepped by the dead man lying on the ground, but she knew she had to focus on the fight. She had gotten weaker, softer. It could have been a fatal mistake. The woman charged towards her and pushed her on the ground. She lifted up her fist wrapped in a metal plate. If she hit her, she could die in minutes. Then she thought why not? What does she have left in this world? Her parents abandoned her, she lost her best friend and she didn´t have any money. Again, North passed through her mind.

"I shouldn't have made that damn promise"

She said aloud and grabbed the woman´s lifted hand. She was stronger than she looked. She couldn´t hold it much longer. Years of being a slave didn´t help her. She dug her broken nails deep into her skin until the woman moved the hand away and pushed it towards her face. The thing she didn't realise was the knife Jade had grabbed in the meantime. Her hand ran along the sharp steel of her knife. The skin tore from her wrist to the elbow. She opened her fist and looked at the deep wound. Her face was covered in blood and it made Jade gag. The woman had realised what happened seconds earlier. She let out a fearful cry and collapsed on her while sobbing. It shook her to the core.

"I´m sorry. I´m so sorry" She sobed into her shirt.

"No. I´m sorry." Said the woman and tears started falling from her eyes.

"At least Andras will leave us alone now." She sobbed.

"Who is Andras?"

"The guy that's still alive. He kept us two in his cages. Thank you for saving me."

"No!" Jade yelled and took a piece of rope. She wrapped it around her arm and made a tight knot.

She looked at her straight in the eyes. "Look I don't know what Andras did to you but you can´t give up because of it. You have a new life now. Run!"

"Thank you a thousand times." She squeezed her hand and ran off.

"Wow Alya! After all I gave you!" Andras jelled and ran after her.

"Hey Andras you bastard! What are you? Scared of me?" She yelled at him and waved her hands.

He looked at her and slowly started walking in her direction. She started running over the roofs. He followed her and they ran across bridges, balconies and roofs. Suddenly a huge gap appeared before her. She got dizzy when she looked down. Andras was running right behind her so she closed her eyes, took a few large steps back and started sprinting. On the edge, she pushed her body forward and jumped. She could see the street below her. The jump felt like ages. Suddenly she felt her feet hit the ground. She fell and rolled over so her back hit the wall. She opened her eyes and saw Andras in the air gripping his knife. Her heart stopped for a minute as he caught himself on the edge of the building.

"Please help me!" He yelled.

"Why should I help you? You tried to kill me!"

"Kill you? No! I was trying to talk to you! What did Alya tell you?" he yelled in response.

"She said you keep people in captivity!" Her voice trembled.

"Little brat. I run a prison for people working as hitmen. They ran away today morning."

"And why should I trust you?" she raised her eyebrows.

"Here, take my knife." He let go of the knife he was holding. She picked it up and took a good look at it. It looked gorgeous. Its light blue blade had a white gradient over it and the handle fit perfectly to her hand.

"Give me your hand." She said and reached down. She pulled him up and they both sat on the ground and breathed loudly. Andras was wearing a grey hoodie and some black pants. His skin was fair, his hair was black and eyes grey. He looked rather cute. He was similar to dust. What happened to Dust? How could she just ran off without him? But she missed him. Oh, she missed him so bad.

"Thank you for that." Andras´s voice cut through the thick silence.

"No problem man." She replied slowly.

"No seriously, I owe you." He smiled.

"It´s okay. No hard feelings." She reached out her hand and they make an awkward handshake-like move.

"My name is Jade."

"Nice to meet you Jade." He said and smiled. She blushed a little and looked down.

He pulled a bottle of water from his backpack and took it to his mouth. Instead of drinking, he turned to her.

"You want some?"

"Yes please!" She was thirsty as hell. She took the bottle and took a few large sips of cold, refreshing water. It was an amazing relief. She got up

"I have to go find North" She put her arms to her hips.

"I can help you!" He jumped up

"Thank you so much." She said and smiled. She may have finally found a friend for her. Maybe something more. But no. She could never forget Dust.

Wasteland

"I think he went that way" She pointed her finger across the roofs to her left. She took a few steps. Her legs felt heavy.

"What the hell?" She said loudly to herself.

"You know. I didn't think you were that dumb. I really thought you wouldn't drink it." Her mind spun. How could he? She tried to walk away but her legs wouldn´t hold her. Her vision got blurry. She really was dumb to ever trust anyone. She hoped he wouldn´t go after North. The thoughts left her petrified. She tried to fight against the tiredness. Tears stared filling her eyes.

"I hate...y...you!" She managed to say with difficulty.

„Ha ha ha, you're so cute when you're helpless!" He grabbed her hand and she quickly put it away. She walked a few steps forward and tripped to her knees. She was almost there. She just had to run. She could make it. She got up and tried to run but fell down. She caught herself with her hands. Andras walked over to her.

„Don't be scared baby." his voice was disgusting. He leaned down and roughly grabbed her chin. He pulled her face up to look at it and then turned it quickly to the side.

„Oh yeah! You're a real trophy!" it made her gag. What was she thinking? And suddenly it all went black. She couldn´t see, she couldn´t hear but she could felt Andras picking her up. That was the last thing she felt.

She slowly opened her eyes. She could feel the cold hard ground against her back. Her hand hurt but she wasn´t sure why. Her eyes slowly adjusted to the bright light above her head. It was a blue light next the one that wasn´t working. She slowly started remembering what happened. The guys, the fight, the wound on her hand. And Andras! That snapped her back to reality and she regained sensation of her body. She shot her head up and saw Andras. His cold fingers were pushing against her arm and his hand was gripping her hip. She screamed and pushed him off her. She could see he was shocked. He didn't expect her waking up.

„Damn it woman! You ruined it!" He groaned.

„You´re sick in the head! How could you do that?" She shouted at his face.

„I just couldn't resist you!" he said and grabbed her wrist. She tried to resist but her hands were still weak. He pushed her against the wall.

„So you want it rough?" He grinned, flashing his yellow teeth.

„I want to roughly drive a knife into your head!" She screamed and resisted but she couldn´t escape his grip.

„You aren't getting out of this baby!" he got his face close to hers. His breath stunk of blood. What the hell was this man doing with blood? He pushed his ice cold lips against her cheek. It made her scream.

„Let me go! I hate you! Leave me alone!"

„Do I look like I care sweetheart?" She had to do something quickly. She couldn´t let him do this to her. And as he pushed his fingers into her mouth she bit. She bit as hard as she could. And managed to bite off his finger. He yelled at her and moved away. She had blood in her mouth left so she spit it to his face and ran.

The room was dark and empty. There was a table and a small cage with a human arm in the left corner. Jade´s stomach turned at the sight of it but she had to get away. On the table, she could see her knife but she needed her backpack too. She looked around and it was on Andras´s back. He was turned the other way, bandaging his fingers so she threw the knife at him. He fell down but he was still alive. She walked over to give him the final stab. But she wondered... he did this to her. He wasn´t worthy enough to die. She ripped her backpack of off his body and dragged him over to the cage. She locked it and threw the key out.

„So you've done it huh?" He grinned.

„What do you want?"

„I loved you... But I guess you aren't worth being loved."

„You don't know shit about love bastard!" She said and walked out. She slammed locked the door behind her.

Wasteland

She walked along the big hallway. The building seemed to be large but completely empty. She had to try to find some resources, so she searched. The rooms, hallways, closets. And all she found were some pictures. There was Andras in all of them. Beside him, there was a girl. They looked happy. But as she looked at more, the girl seemed to be weaker and weaker by every one of the pictures. The last photo was Andras with the man she killed and Alya. He looked almost depressed. she could almost feel sorry for him. Almost. Jade walked on to try and find the exit. She walked for minutes but she just couldn´t seem to find it. She was sick of this building! She just had to get out! She needed to find North! She took an old wooden plank and threw it at a window. When she saw the smashed glass, fear ran through her body. She closed her eyes and memories flashed through her mind. She had to stop this. She couldn´t be afraid of glass and limit herself with it. So she picked up a little piece and carved symbol on her hand. It was some sort of rune she read about in an old book. It was supposed to represent bravery. Sure, it hurt, but her fear was gone. Although she realised the stupidity in carving stuff in her skin. It was dangerous and she could get seriously infected. I'll never do that again. She thought.

She climbed out the window. The surroundings were completely new to her. Who knew how far from her shelter she was. She circled the building a few times and tried to find some sort of clue. When she circled the building for the third time, she caught a glimpse of herself in a window. There was blood on her face and a wound on her hand she looked awful. She will never kill again. She couldn´t handle it anymore. She washed herself with cold water from a river nearby and let it run down her hands. It was sad how scarred her body got overtime. Cuts, broken bones, torn muscles. But after all, she was still alive and quite healthy. She turned around and set off. She needed to find North.

CHAPTER 11: Shattered Trust

Wasteland

CHAPTER 12

Memories of a Broken Child

CHAPTER 12: Memories of a Broken Child

On the path, she saw blood stains. They could be hers, so she followed them to a big tree. There were names carved in it. They were all crossed except hers, Alya´s and Jet´s. He must have been that other guy. After all, the tree was just as much of a bad sight as it was a good one. She was on the right path. She continued walking. She walked past skyscrapers, houses and parks all broken down and overgrown by vines. She stopped from time to time to rest and look at the surroundings. The world was amazing. So many shapes and materials. She wondered what it was like in the beginning. She wondered how the universe was created. How can something just appear from almost nothing? What does nothing look like? People knew so much but they were so dumb compared to everything that hasn't been discovered yet. She looked up to the sky and the first stars had already appeared. She smiled slightly and laid down on a wooden bench to her right. She closed her eyes and fell asleep in moments. She woke up in the middle of the night to a weird scratching sound. It seemed like small footsteps. She quickly opened her eyes and saw a tiny Aiwan in front of her. Aiwans were small monkey- like creatures with yellow feathers poking from their big ears. They came in many different colours. White, red, blue and so on. This one was Blue and white. It was beautiful! She took her backpack and took out some of the dried fruit she had left. She took a handful and reached her hand out. The Aiwan came forward, took 2 and ran off. She never thought she would see one of these in her life. She laid back down and fell asleep again. The night was cold but calm and peaceful.

The sun woke her up early in the morning. Her back hurt from the uncomfortable sleeping position. She opened her eyes slowly. The sun was blinding. When her eyes adjusted to the sunlight, she slowly sat up. There, in front of her, was sitting the Aiwan she saw last night. It tilted its head to the side and made a curious clicking noise. She threw him another piece of fruit. She smiled and stood up to start walking again. She had to find North. What if something happened to him? She bet he was hungry. She speeded up her walking. After quite some time she heard footsteps behind her. She grabbed her knife and darted around ready to attack. But all she could see was that same Aiwan again.

"Oh. I´m sorry buddy. I didn't mean to scare you." She stretched out her hand.

"Come on. We don't have much time." The Aiwan ran to her arm and hopped on it. It´s eyes were big and bright. She petted his head and sat it on her shoulder.

"You need a name buddy. What should I call you?" They walked past a store and she read.

"Pay less, Buy more! PB...that sounds very unique! Hmmmm Pop Bubble.....Papaya...no! That's dumb...let's call you Zmey." She said and petted his tiny head. After a few hours of walking, she noticed a familiar building.

She ran out in the street and Zmey was following right behind. He jumped on her shoulder. She started walking to the place where she split up with North. She walked past buildings she knew since she was 6. A restaurant she used to eat in. She had the same meal every single time. Mashed potatoes with cauliflower meat nuggets. It seemed weird but actually it was finger licking good! A bit forward there was a school she used to go in. She had fun there. It´s where she met her best friend Avery. The school was segregated on two parts. The normal kids and the ˜unwants˜ like they used to call them. Avery was a part of the normal children but didn't mind hanging out with the other part. She was always kind and caring. Her hair was coloured blue and pink. Jade could remember her so clearly. Her eyes were dark brown. She was wearing glasses. The large nerdy ones. She always teased her about it. They had such a good time together. Her memory flashed back to the first time she stepped into this school. She sat down on an old swing and let her memories flow. It felt like flying through her mind. Her heartbeat slowed down and her breathing got deeper. Suddenly, she was standing in front of the school gates, gripping the straps on her bag. It wasn´t real, but it felt real. Like she shifted herself into a memory. The edges of her vision were foggy but it all felt so real. She could feel, hear and probably even taste and smell. She pushed the gates. They felt heavy. Her 6 year old self didn't have much strength. When she walked in everyone stared at her. It freaked her out. Some were even laughing at her. She wanted to beat the crap out of them, but she would never do that back then. She kept walking and looking to the ground until she bumped into something. She looked up and saw a man´s face.

"Hello sweetheart. Where are you going?" He asked her in a polite tone.

"I´m not sure." She said quietly.

"Come with me" he said. They entered a large room full of kids.

"They are all new. Just like you." Said the man with a smile on his face. She sat on a free spot text to a girl. She pulled her sleeve.

"Hey! Stop that" Jade shouted and pulled her hand away.

"Oh. I´m sorry. I just wanted to ask your name. I´m Avery and I´m eight and a half years old. Who are you?" She said with a big smile on her face.

"I´m Jade." she said quietly.

"Cool! You look like a fun girl! I hope we get in class together!"

"I...guess." She was really bright and happy all the time. That was what she always liked about her. Suddenly, she snapped back to her real self. She didn´t open her eyes and kept swinging and enjoying the cold air brushing her face.

She didn´t know how her and Avery became friends, but she guessed Avery just kept talking to her and she eventually trusted her. But she never had any idea how much she would end up meaning to her. They always dreamed about how they´ll save the world and find guys for themselves. About exploring the sewers and going on epic trips. She remembered their first sleepover. Avery had great supporting parents that didn't mind looking after her. They were like sisters. They shared everything with each other. They used to sing songs so loud that you couldn't hear the music anymore. They even made themselves matching necklaces. Maybe they were just good friends because they were both training to become warriors. But warriors of Ixah had it way easier. A brief smile painted across her lips.

And she could remembered the time Avery told her she was sick.

She wasn't sick on her body but she didn't understand at that time. She was way too young. It was late. One am. Neither them could sleep so they were just talking.

"So Jade. I have something to tell you."

"Oh yeah?" jade jumped up and getting closer to her,

"I have something."

"We all do!" She said jokingly but Avery´s eyes remained serious.

"Oh... Well go on then." She looked concerned and visibly swallowed.

"The doctor said it´s a disorder. She was saying stuff like ~attention~ and ~stress~. I didn't really understand. She said I have schizophrenia. It´s when people can´t tell or understand what´s real and what isn´t. It causes hallucinations. That means I see and hear things that aren't real. It usually leads to anxiety or depression, but don't worry. They gave me some medicine and I should be alright." She looked at Jade, kind of embarrassed with a ~please don't think I'm weird look~.

"It´s okay" Jade said and smiled at her. It will end up being okay. She was sure. She tried to sound as supportive as she could. They never really talked about it afterwards. The pills seemed to help her. After a few months or so, she thought it was fine and stopped taking them. Jade surely didn't like her choice, but Avery said they were making her tired. She did look weak, but Jade never thought it wasn't normal. She never ate much anyway. Jade noticed her mom was down lately too. In a week, her hallucinations came back. She would find her in the middle of the night screaming at a wall. She tried to help but she couldn't. She would wake up and cry while saying:

"Red, Black, Red, Black...." Repeatedly.

One night she shook her awake with a pale face and a look of terror on it.

"Please help me!" She looked at her and nothing seemed off except a bite mark on her hand.

"Who did that to you!?" Jade shouted.

Wasteland

"It was... the woman! She won´t leave!" Avery cried.

Finally, she realised. There was no woman.

"Avery there is no woman in here. You need your medicine now!" she rushed over to her bedtable and scrambled for a blue liquid and a syringe. She had no idea how to handle it, so she had to improvise. She ran back to her and almost shouted.

"Hold still." Avery did as she said but was still shaking in fear. jade stood there for a moment, thinking how to do it and then she just stabbed her in the arm. Her body absorbed the liquid and eventually she calmed down. Jade couldn't sleep that night. It was crazy.

The next day they were planning a trip to the lake with her parents. It was Saturday. Avery was back to normal and taking her medication. They were all sitting in the kitchen to eat breakfast. Her mom was very relaxed and open-minded. She was into hippies and old music. Unlike her dad. He was a salesperson at a company that was selling technological wonders all over Ixah. Her mom Nadya was the first to notice Avery´s bite.

"What happened?" She asked concerned, but calm.

"I´m sorry...I thought I was okay but I guess I'm not." Mumbled Avery.

"Did you stop taking your pills?" Her dad raised his eyebrows.

"I did...I'm really sorry." Then her dad went crazy.

"This was entirely your fault Jade! You were supposed to protect her! You were her friend!"

"Dad! She still is!" Yelled Avery.

"Don't say that! Tell her why she is here instead! Tell her you are only her friend so she can take care of you!"

"That's not true!" jade just sat there with tears falling down her face.

"Avery could die and you are to fault!" Nadya tried to calm him down but nothing worked.

"I told you orphans can´t be equal to people! Even their own parents didn't want them. What were you thinking Avery?!" Jade´s head fell into her palms.

"Dad please stop!" Cried Avery.

CHAPTER 12: Memories of a Broken Child

"Get out of my house Jade!" He yelled at the top of his lungs.

"I´m really sorry" She mumbled, stood up and walked through the door leaving tiny puddles behind her. She left everything in that home. Her soul, her happiness and some of her stuff. But looking back, she guessed he was right. Even her own parents didn't want her. She snapped out of her thoughts and she was back, sitting in the swing. That was the last time she saw Avery. She was not sad about it anymore, but she hoped she´s doing okay.

78

CHAPTER 13

Reconnected

CHAPTER 13: Reconnected

She could hear some children talking behind her. A man and a woman were lifting children from a black van to the ground.

"Come on guys. Let´s go." They looked like good people.

"Jade! Jadeee!" A soft voice woke her from her thoughts.

"North!?" A tiny head popped from the group and ran towards her. The white hair shone in the sun. It was him! Her heart jumped a little. And she sighed in relief.

"Where were you Jade?" He looked upset.

"I am so sorry buddy. Some weird guys took me away."

"I missed you Jade." She smiled.

"Aww I missed you too little guy." She looked back at the group. They didn't notice he was gone.

"What´s sitting on your shoulder?" He asked curiously.

"That´s our new friend Zmey." She smiled at him.

"Hello Zmey!"

"Let´s go quickly." She said and they ran through the streets. She noticed Avery´s house from the distance and paused. She just had to go in. Jade thought to herself.

"North here!" She shouted and held the door open for him.

It´s been 4 years since she was last in here. The flat still looked the same. Yellow walls with green patterns. Avery´s room was upstairs. She still had the same furniture. She recalled memories of the gentle pastel blue wall. They used to draw on it a lot. She walked over to the wall and noticed some letters. ~Avery & Jade = BFF~ It seemed such a long time ago. She looked over to North. He was sitting on the floor, watching a doll. The room was very messy. There were things laying all over the place. Clothes, pills, bed sheets.

"Who´s there!?" A voice from another room shouted.

"North hide. " She whispered. He jumped in a closet and held Zmey as she stood behind the door gripping her knife. She could hear footsteps going upstairs. She followed the sound to the attic.

It was messy and dust was all over the place. Old crap was all over the place. Jade remembered it much cleaner. She used to come up there with Avery to play dress-ups with her mom´s clothes. The large mirror was still there. She could almost see them laughing, pretending to be old ladies walking around a castle. However, enough of that. She looked around to find whatever she followed up there. She saw a small door at the other end. It was wide open. Her only idea was to squeeze through it. She found herself standing on a flat roof. She never knew that was there. She looked around and saw a person standing in a corner looking down on the street. Black ripped jeans and a white top.

"Hey you!" She shouted at the person. They turned around and then she saw it. The glasses, Pink-blue hair and fair skin.

"Avery!" She shouted out. She seemed distracted and careless. Avery turned back to look at the street and Jade pulled her hand. What was she doing? The girl's eyes were filled with tears and her voice trembled as she spoke.

"I need ro end it. The voices won't stop. Leave me alone!" Jade's heart dropped and she almost felt crushed by the heavy words.

"You need a good rest girl." She said to Avery but also herself. She stared into her eyes and hugged her. She really missed her.

"Don´t worry. It´s me, Jade." She collapsed into her lap and shook her head, but didn´t say a word. She quietly helped her get up and walked over to her bed. She laid down and stared at the ceiling.

"Jade the woman was here all the time. She still is." Avery said confused.

"Where is your medicine Avery?"

"In the wonder world. I went there yesterday." She smiled wide.

"That doesn't sound good." North stepped out of the closet, looking scared to death.

"It´s okay buddy. Wait here ok?" She said and stood up. He just nodded. She opened a drawer on Avery´s bedtable. It was full of empty bottles.

"No luck. Avery do you have any medicine left?" She asked with a shaking voice. She didn't want her to get worse. She didn't answer.

Wasteland

She entered the bathroom and opened a white cabinet above the sink. There were all sorts of medicine and luckily the blue one too, but no syringes. It´ll have to do. She said to herself and walked back. Avery was laying on the bed, laughing at herself.

"This may hurt a little." Jade said and pulled her sleeve up. She took out her knife and made a tiny cut on her wrist. She pressed the bottle to the cut and waited. Avery slowly started saying normal things and calmed down.

"Jade. What are you doing here?" She blinked a few times.

"Don't talk. Sleep." She answered and started bandaging Avery´s arm.

"What happened to her? Asked North curiously.

"She was a little sick. She just needed her medicine. She will be okay." She calmed him down. Avery fell asleep, they walked downstairs, and she searched the kitchen.

"Did you ever eat cereal North?" She asked him.

"What is cereal?"

"You´ll see." She laughed. She poured him some milk and a few spoons of cereal that she found in a drawer. He was munching on it when they heard rustling upstairs. Jade ran to Avery´s room and blasted the door open.

"Avery! How are you?" She almost shouted.

"What?" Avery looked confused.

"It´s me! How are you feeling? I´m happy to see you again!" She just looked at Jade, confused.

"Jade?" she carefully replied.

"That´s me!" She smiled and Avery jumped up and gave her a tight hug.

Her eyes filled with excitement. "Where were you?"

"Everywhere basically." Jade laughed back

"Is that your kiddo?" She asked, pointing behind Jade. She turned around and saw North peeking from behind the door.

"He´s my little sidekick." She said and held his hand to pull him closer. Avery looked at her bandaged hand.

"What happened to me?" She asked worried.

"Well. You kind of went crazy." Jade´s smile faded.

"Ow. Yeah. Sorry about that." Avery looked down.

Jade was curious. She had to know more. "So what happened?"

"I ran out of pills. I thought it was time for me to die. Thank you for coming over."

"No problem." She managed to squeeze out of herself. She wanted to know what went on after she left so she asked.

"So what was your life like?"

"Oh it was great!" Avery said, but she saw her eyes lose the spark. Jade sat down beside her and took her hand

"Now tell me the truth please."

"After you left it all went downhill for me. I lost interest in every-thing. My father started drinking and blamed it on my sickness. It was crashing our family. One day he disappeared and never came back. Osen later invaded the street and my mom was killed. I man-aged to survive somehow. I continued living here alone. It´s been 2 years and a month but I'm getting better. Medicine was the only problem. So I'm stuck here till Axel returns."

"Axel?" Jade raised her eyebrows.

"Ow yeah. I didn't tell you. He´s my fiancé"

"Wow. Congrats!" Jade smiled.

"Thank you. I really missed you, you know. I will never forgive myself for not standing up for you." Avery sighed.

"Don't worry about it." Jade said awkwardly. She was never really good with people. She patted Avery on the shoulder while she continued to talk.

"I and axel are planning to live in the forest. It should be much safer than here. He went there to build shelter a week ago. OH. I didn't even tell you what he looks like! He has dark skin and black hair. His eyes are gray. It´s amazing how close we grew over the past year. He gave me the most beautiful ring!" She said and carefully stretched her hand in front of her, to reveal a shiny rose gold ring with a sapphire flower stone in the middle.

"Wow! It seems like you two really like each other." jade said almost offended because she felt like Avery was only replacing her.

"Yeah. I was sick of living here in the past. I need freedom and happiness." She could feel sadness slowly crawl in her head at the thought of Avery leaving again.

"Do you want to stay over for a few days?" Avery asked and snapped Jade out of her head.

"Uh. Yeah, sure." She said confused.

"Hey North. I have some toys for you." She said. North´s mouth stretched from one ear to another. Avery flipped over an old box and toys fell on the floor. North started exploring and Zmey curiously joined him. Avery then walked over to a table and piced up what looked like 2 pieces of string.

"Here." She said and handed Jade one. There was a small metal plate on both of them.

"Till all the stars burn out." Avery read aloud.

"I´ll be your friend." Jade read from the other.

"You saved them." She looked down and smiled.

"Of course I did! We worked damn hard on them!" They both laughed. They both slipped them on their wrists and she could almost feel like they were kids again. But they changed and grew up. Heavy silence filled the room and moments felt like hours. Finally, Avery´s voice cut tough the thick air.

"We should eat something!"

"Great idea." Jade said and saw Zmey curiously lift his head up. She reached in her pocket and gave him a few seeds. All four of them headed downstairs. Avery opened the fridge and pulled out some meat. Jade´s jaw probably dropped through the floor. When Avery saw her, she started laughing insanely loud. They spent the next few hours recalling memories, singing and having fun. Like the good old days. She missed being friends with her. She was still as cool as 4 years ago. But on the inside she still felt empty and dull. She knew that in reality she was still alone. Avery moved on, she didn´t need her at all. She had someone to take care of her, to support her. Jade never thought she was that weak. But at moments like this she wished she could have somebody to be strong for her. Since she found North she couldn´t show him that she was scared. She had to make sure he was all right.

The day passed and they didn't do much. She had to admit that she missed sleeping in a bed. North was enjoying all the toys. He probably hadn't seen them in a while.

Jade could barely sleep. She kept waking up in the middle of the night to a sound of people walking outside. She wasn´t used to it. The streets around the shelter were never busy. Every little sound caused her to dart out of bed and search for her knife. She felt disappointed, defeated even. She had become a wreck. Her mind and body were a mess. She couldn't afford to be nervous and stressed. The night passed. Slowly.

Wasteland

CHAPTER 14

Swimming in Sadness

CHAPTER 14: Swimming in Sadness

Confused, she looked around the room. It was almost morning already. She decided she had enough sleep and walked downstairs. As her feet hit the stairs, a heavenly smell filled her nose.

"What is that?" She said and walked on. Avery was standing behind the kitchen counter making waffles.

"It´s been years since I last tasted waffles!" She screamed, almost drooling over herself.

"Well don't wait then. They will get cold!" She smiled and sat at the neatly arranged table. She took a spoon of honey and spread it over the hot waffle. She cut into its crispy crust. It was soft and buttery. She had always loved waffles. Her mom used to make them every Sunday. It was like a tradition to her. She loved it. North came down as well. They were all sitting at the table, chatting and laughing. She let her guards down completely. It felt like she was at the right place. Things were starting to look brighter. She found North, she reunited with a lost friend. Nothing could ruin this moment for her. After some time she might feel hopeful again. But it was just a moment.

A loud bang on the door snapped jade back to reality.

"Axel!" Shouted Avery and ran towards him.

"You are back already!" She smiled. Instead of hugging her, he pushed her on the floor. His eyes looked red and angry He had a large body dressed in green pants and a black shirt. He walked over to North and Jade.

"Stop it right there!" Shouted Avery.

"Who are they!? What did they do to you!?" His voice was deep.

"Nothing! Jade is my lost friend!" Avery yelled at him.

"You brought strangers into our home!? They aren't even clean blood!" He sounded furious.

"We went through this."

"Look at the little hybrid rat!" He was talking about North. Jade knew he was different. She didn´t know if she should be excited or scared. Hybrids could be quite dangerous. They often had supernatural abilities. Axel had obviously done some military work judging by his shape. Plus the military hates hybrids.

"North run!" She screamed as loud as possible, but he didn´t react. She looked over to him.

"North please. We have to go now. We can´t stay here. Please!" But he didn't move a muscle. Before she managed to say anything else, Axel knocked her down. She took a few seconds to get up and breathe, but it was too late. He took North and Avery away. Probably to a military station. She couldn´t just stand there and do nothing. She ran outside and saw a military car driving down the street. She remembered Avery´s dad owning a motorcycle. She picked up Zmey and ran to the garage.

"Yes! You are still here!" She shouted and jumped on the bike. She didn't have the keys. Trying not to waste time she cut some random wires and hoped for the best. She felt like some kind of movie star when the bike grunted a little bit. To her disappointment it didn't start. She ran out on the street and searched the surroundings. She needed to find a car or something quickly.

"Score!" jade shouted out when she saw the blue parking lot sign ahead of her. She ran to the nearest car and looked inside.

"No keys. Great!" She searched the lot but none of the cars had keys in them. Suddenly she heard a rustling sound behind her.

"Zmey! You found the keys!" She grabbed the old rusty keys and pressed the button. A creepy broken beeping sound filled the air. She turned around and looked at the beeping car. A light was broken. It was brown and looked somewhat like a mountain car. There was a place for a spare tire, but it was empty. The glass was broken, but it had to do. She opened the rusty door and sat on the driver´s seat. Zmey jumped to the seat next to her and started playing with a golden charm hanging from the roof fof the car.

"And let there be gas." Jade said jokingly and turned the key. The car grunted and stopped.

"Come on!" She shouted and hit the steering wheel. The car grunt-

Wasteland

ed again and started up.

"Yes!" She threw her arms in the air and held the wheel.

"Now we pray I´ll figure out how to drive this thing." She stepped on the pedal and drove across the broken asphalt. The car was unsteady, but she somehow managed to make a turn. She floored it, driving along the long straight road. She loved the wind in her hair and the cold breeze on her cheeks. She sang to a song on the radio to ignore the fact North could be dead by now. It was a song from a band she had always loved. She never knew their name, but it was a rock band.

"But after all, I´m still standing tall.

With one hand on my chest and the other on your back.

But this isn´t a love song,

Isn´t a love song!

I´m gonna push you away and free myself from the cage.

With one hand on my chest and the other high in the air!

Man, she love these songs!"

A brown sign was hovering above the road ahead of her. Military 100m //CAUTION//

"Get ready Zmey! Stuff will go down!" jade stopped the car in front a large wall. She stepped on the ground and slammed the door shut. Luckily, there were no soldiers near and there was a small opening on the gates. It was just big enough for her to squeeze trough. She stepped towards the gates and looked up. The large wall was similar to the one on the edge of the city. It was at least 8m tall and covered in white sprayed numbers. She was not sure what they meant, nor she really cared. She sneaked through the opening and Zmey jumped after her.

"No Zmey! Wait here!" He looked at her with his sad eyes and sat down.

She petted his head and turned to the base. It was worn down and poorly armed. All of the soldiers were probably transmitted to other bases to attack the upper layer in Vigrior, leaving this base with terrible protection. A hissing sound dragged her attention to the inner door. A solider stepped out and she hid behind the wall. She needed to find a way to hold the door open quickly. She grabbed a rock and threw it at the door. It started to close, but bumped against the hard object and opened again. She ran towards and slipped through the thick metal door.

Inside, there were three hallways. One on the left, one on the right and the one jade was standing in. She could hear two voices yelling from her left.

"You betrayed me!"

"I just wanted to help..." Sobbed the softer voice. It was Avery´s. The other one must be Axel.

"I don't care!"

"I´m sorry..."

"You better be! Hybrids are no joke!"

"I´m sorry. I didn't know."

"What do you know? Look sorry I got mad. Let´s leave."

"Okay. I love you."

"I love you too."

Traitors. Jade thought to herself. She could hear the gates open and footsteps walking away. A sudden yell teared the air.

"Yo Haylo! Make sure you give the Hybrid it´s pills. And get rid of him soon enough!"

"Sure thing commander!" a woman shouted back.

Jade ran towards the cells she saw on her left. There! A patch of white hair on the bed. It was North! She got her knife and started picking the lock. She was well aware that the woman heard her and was coming. The footsteps got louder and jade had no luck with the lock. She turned around and saw Haylo running towards her. Her skin was dark as night but her hair was bright blue. She looked quite stunning. She turned back to check on North. He was standing there. Still. His eyes were fully black. He looked terrifying.

„North! Are you okay?" She shouted at him and shook the bars.

Wasteland

Nothing. Suddenly, she could feel a light breeze and moments later the metal bars knocked her down and pinned her to the wall. She lost her breath for a second. North stepped out of the cell and faced the woman. She had a katana sword it was black and red. The blade shone every time she passed a light. She threw the sword towards North.

„North watch out!" jade yelled as loud as she could, still trapped against the wall. The sword was now a step away from him. And then it stopped in mid-air right before his forehead. North lifted up his eyes in the katana crumbled to tiny pieces. The woman yelled and charged forward. She jumped on his tiny body and sliced his arm with a knife.

„No! North!" jade cried out.

„I hate you!" She shouted at the woman. Cold tears ran down her heated cheeks. The woman stood up and grinned at her. In the meantime, North slowly got up and launched the knife at the woman. She was shocked. Her eyes filled with horror and she started coughing blood. She collapsed to her knees and cried out. When jade realized what had happened she tried to free herself. She pushed her legs against the metal bars and her back at the wall. The bars slowly moved, so she pushed harder. The steel structure finally moved after a minute and fell over. She fell to the ground with a ghasping thud and ran towards North´s motionless body. His hand was bleeding really bad.

"Think, think, think!" Jade told herself. She grabbed her belt and tied it above the wound. It wasn´t really helping. She cried out and hugged her little friend. One of his eyes was normal, but the other one was still black. Her hands were shaking as she brushed his hair aside with her blood-covered hand.

"What´s happening." She heard a tiny voice. Tears ran down her face, but she tried to speak calmly.

"You´re dreaming buddy. You´re okay." She sniffed.

"Why are you crying?" He asked and looked at his arm. His eyes filled with tears.

"Am I dying?" His tiny voice was trembling.

"No! No. You´ll just fall asleep okay?" She took him in her arms and stroked his hair.

"And tomorrow we can go swimming." jade smiled at him gently and wiped her nose.

"I always wanted to go swimming." He tried to smile back. Jade knew he won´t make it, but she didn't want him to lose hope. He was too young and gentle. Life isn´t fair! No! She won´t let him die. She gripped him tighter.

"I promise to look over you." He said. The words pierced into Jade´s heart like a knife. He didn't look sad or in pain. Just scared. She failed to protect him. Just like Dust. She was a failure.

"Don't worry little guy. I promise to find you and then we will go swimming." He was slowly closing his eyes. She couldn't help it but cry. She spoke with her voice shaking.

"I´ve had tons of great days with you North. I want to tell you you´re amazing and the best sidekick I could ever wish for." His grip on her hand got loose and his eyes slowly shut. She put her shaking hand on his chest. His heart wasn´t beating anymore. She burred her face in her palms and let out an animal-like scream. She never cried that much before. It felt like millions of razor sharp knives shattered her chest into pieces.

She was not sure for how long she sat there. It could be an hour. She couldn´t just leave him here to rot. She searched the base and found a blanket. She wrapped and carried the tiny fragile now life-less North outside. Zmey was happily jumping around and chasing flies. She circled the area and noticed a lake nearby. The grass was incredibly green compared to others. It almost didn´t look yellow. There were even some orchids growing on it. She walked down and laid North on the meadow next to it. She started picking flowers. How could anyone kill a helpless child? People are horrible. And he was everything to her. She had a purpose. What was she supposed to do now? Who will she care about? It was almost evening already. She had a large bouquet in her hands. Red and white orchids. She laid the flowers next to North. The so-called cleaning services will take care of the body. She walked to the water and sat down. The sun was going down, creating a clash of colors.

Wasteland

Red, purple, blue and turquoise all mixed up to create a stunning masterpiece. She stared at the water. She thought she was crying, but she wasn't sure anymore. She just hoped North was doing well. She would never forget him. No. She will always remember. She gently smiled and wiped a tear from her cheek. Once again, she had everything taken away from her.

"Look North. You can go swimming now."

CHAPTER 15

A New Beginning

CHAPTER 15: A New Beginning

It had been a week since North´s death. She had been trying to find her place in life again and to get herself together. She returned to where they spent most of their time. Her old shelter. It was now completely torn down. Half of the roof collapsed. The chest had holes in it. Mice probably made them, but she missed her home. She spent a couple of days just lying around, doing nothing. Till yesterday. Now she had enough of wasting her life. It was the only one she had. She couldn't afford to lay around and do nothing. So she grabbed her backpack and turned it around above the mattress in the hope to find her purpose. She searched everything. Some seeds, paper, a pencil and that weird tree of ruins drive. She made a choice right there at the moment. She carefully climbed down, plugged in the laptop and loaded the drive. She typed

--APPLY—

It took her to the mission list and then directly to the one she was invited to. The title said:

[HUMMINGIRD 001263// **STARTING TIME: 12DAYS21HOURS13SECONDS**]

She opened the mission and a window popped up.

[ACCEPT/DENY]

Jade clicked accept with a shaking hand and it took her to another page.

[PLEASE FILL IN: EYE SCAN//FINGERPRINT SCAN]

The directions guided her through complex procedures to the eye and fingerprint scans. When it was done, coordinates flashed on her screen. She took a pen and wrote them down on her hand, 014ep812zxy. The drive then closed and she was left with her heart pounding and short on her breath. She applied to a war mission. And it was supposed to be against Osen. She didn't have anything better to do anyway. Therefore, she packed her backpack, entered the coordinates into a map on the laptop and threw herself in the car. She looked out and saw Zmey looking at her. She just couldn't leave him there. No! Zmey was coming with her!

So now they were here. Driving on the highway, singing songs and laughing at stupid radio shows full of propaganda. She was still thinking about North. She hoped he was happy now, but she guessed she'll never know. She never believed in ghosts. The laptop next to Zmey on the passenger´s seat was showing her the map. They were about halfway there. The car was almost out of gas. They´ve been driving for 5 hours already. Good thing there was a town ahead of them. They drove through the large gate and she spotted a huge banner above a large building.

"MARKET WORLD!"

Without thinking, she pulled the car over to the building.

"Zmey! Let´s have some fun!" She shouted and ran inside feeling like a kid on Christmas morning.

There were clothes, some interior, food, accessories and everything she had ever dreamed of! And the best thing about it? It was abandoned! First, she ran to the food stand and stuffed her mouth with chocolates. She walked over to the snacks and filled her backpack with cookies, chips and other snacks. There, on the floor was a gun. She picked it up and tucked it behind her belt just in case. Next, she ran to the beauty products stand. She applied black eyeshadow to her eyelids and put mascara on her lashes. It looked badass! After the makeover, she needed to find new clothes. She walked to the first stand. It was full of classy vests, skirts, and blouses. Not exactly her style. The second shop looked much better! All the clothes were rock styled! She took some awesome looking army pants, took off her shoes and ripped pants. The new ones felt amazing! Comfortable, stretchable and light! She was in heaven! The pants were grey, black, and silver with pockets, chains, and a large belt. Now she needed a top.

"I´m thinking of dark green. What about you Zmey?" She looked over to Zmey and showed him a green long-sleeved turtleneck top. He was playing with necklaces minding his own business.

"Okay!" She said and slipped the top on.

Wasteland

"Now for the jacket. Sure, it's spring, but it still gets cold at night." She thought and walked over to the winter section. She found an oversized light brown jacket. It was so comfortable!

"So that´s it." She stepped in front of a mirror and she looked better than she thought. She still needed a pair of shoes though. Eventually, she found the perfect pair. Black boots with zippers, pins, and laces. They looked awesome!

"Zmey! Are you in for a little fun?" She said jokingly and wiggled her eyebrows. She grabbed the Aiwan and ran to the wooden stroller area. She put him in one and took a head start. After a short sprint, she climbed into the stroller and they were racing across the market, both screaming in fear and excitement. But sadly, her calculations were inaccurate and they crashed into the accessories stand. That gave her an idea.

"I´ll pierce my ears!"

In the back of the store, there were plenty of needles. She stuck one in her ear. The pain was stronger than she expected and it made her jump a bit. But she wasn't weak! She made two holes in her left ear and one in the right. The black subtle earrings looked awesome!

"I love them!" She smiled while admiring herself in the mirror.

She checked out the necklaces next to her. She found half of a heart on a chain. There should be two halves, but one was gone. She took the necklace. It felt like the other part belonged to someone who should be beside her. To Dust maybe. Oh, she missed Dust. She knew it sounded cheesy, but it made her feel like she was meant for something more.

She stepped in the street and looked across the market. It was completely destroyed.

"Oops..." she said carefully and then burst out laughing. Jade and Zmey grabbed some more snacks, she took some extra clothes and then they returned to the car. There were so many on the parking lot she had no problem finding gas. They set off right away.

"We wasted three hours in there!" She said when she looked at the time.

"Totally worth it!" It was fun. She hadn´t had so much fun since she left the home in Shehn a year ago! The sun went down and the moon was slowly rising. The first stars appeared in the sky. She still had three more hours to drive. She liked the nights. They were calm and peaceful. She turned on the music. It was slow and kind of depressing but happy at the same time. A man was singing about letting go and getting better, but he sounded hurt. It made her sad, but he said it all gets better. It always gets better. Things are never as bad as they seem. She closed her eyes for a second to clear her mind. She felt drunk and overwhelmed with feelings. She lost everything but she got hope in return. She was going to war and it brought her a purpose. She was scared but happy. She didn´t have many people to love, but those who she did love loved her back. Life is strange. Some picked hate others love, some turned to drugs others to health. But one thing they all had in common was hiding from reality. They lied, pretended and tried to hide. But what was the reality anyway? They all had their own system that told them what they should and shouldn´t do. She hated systems she hated reality. But who doesn't want to be free? And why did reality limit them? Probably because some people suck. It was understandable. Well nobody will ever find their true purpose, but it didn't really matter. What they had was now. They shouldn't waste it. But oh well. Who was she to talk? She was raised by Arvas. Without family. Without mercy. Her parents hated her. She was an Unwant. She lost everything. And she let down both Dust and North.

She stopped the car. She couldn´t drive in this state. She stepped outside and sat on the grass. Tears flowed through her and cleaned her body of hate. She was left with sadness, hope, and purpose again. She laid down. It was a little cold, but her new jacket was warming her. She watched the stars and the moon looking down on her. She fell asleep like that. It was peaceful and quiet. She didn´t sleep this good in weeks. She missed it. Morning came too quickly. The sun flashed across her face and the dew on the grass was cooling down her hands as she ran them on the ground. She saw Zmey chasing a bee.

Wasteland

She opened a bag of bread snacks and ate them for breakfast. Zmey joined her. They were both hungry from traveling.

"Come on buddy," Jade said and sat in the car. They drove for a few more hours and finally reached their destination. It was a tall grey building.

"Well. That´s it." She said and petted Zmey on the head. She stepped outside shakingly, but she wanted to do it. The gates had a button. She pressed it and waited.

"What do you want?" The strong manly voice pierced her ear. Zmey jumped in her pocket, made a squealing sound and covered his head.

"Hello?" She said hesitantly.

"Go away!" The man almost yelled.

"I´m here to apply for the mission." She said back as calmly as possible.

"Yeah sure. Bullshit! I´m not falling for it again!" He started to get angry.

"I drove for hours to get here! What do you mean bullshit?"

"So what?" She reached her limit.

"Listen up you little brat! I need to get inside the building like it or not!"

"Well get in then!" Yelled the man.

The gates were locked, so she started climbing the fence. It wasn´t that tall, so she could easily cope. She jumped down on the other side and walked over to the main door. It was locked. She didn't have a better idea, so she took out her gun. Clearly, it was a stupid one, but hey! Maybe it works. She took a few steps back closed one eye and aimed for the lock. She hesitated, but you only live once right? She pulled the trigger. After a moment, she heard a deafening bang. The bullet smashed the lock to the point where it almost exploded.

"Well, that was something!" She yelled aloud, raised her fist and pushed the door open with her leg. She stepped into the large round room. There were blinding bright lights on the ceiling. There was a hole in the middle and a fence around it. She looked down and saw several stories deep. The floor was black with light grey stripes all over it.

"Yo! I´m here!" Jade yelled out.

"Don´t brag about it." Said the guy who had just walked in on the other side.

"You´ll get your outfit and the guns, you can sleep on the left with your fancy friends, and food is on the right."

"I´m not fancy?" She replied with a confused face.

"Yeah, whatever. You have the right to stay quiet. This is the army now. I don't want to hear your complaining."

"Yes, sir!" She yelled. He looked at her, confused like she was insane and then left the room.

Wasteland

CHAPTER 16

Yes, Sir!

CHAPTER 16: Yes, Sir!

Jade turned to the left and stared into the corridor in front of her.

"I´m going to break down! I swear!" There was an annoying high pitch voice faking sobbing.

"Oh my god! I´m crying!"

"What the hell is wrong with her?" Jade thought to herself. She slowly started walking towards the room.

"Okay Kylen calm down! You´re being a total crybaby!"

"Well sorry, Abby! I didn't know that old man will sexually harass me!"

"I know right! He was a total sexist! But you need to shut up now!"

"Yeah Khlo nobody wanted to come here"

"Oh really? It was literally your genius idea Kylen!"

Jade stepped in front of the door and it slid open. Suddenly, she was standing in front of three seventeen-year-old girls crying. Their hair was painted in weird rainbow colors and she couldn´t see their faces under the heavy makeup.

"Oh my god hold me!" Yelled one.

"Look at the maid´s outrageous shirt! Her shoes don't match with the mascara!"

"Okay girls. Just calm down." Shouted the other one.

"No Abby! Shut up."

"Yeah shut up and look at her mascara!"

Jade shook her head and said in a fake girly voice as high as possible.

"Heh, actually girls I'm not wearing any makeup!" She saw their jaws drop to the floor and laughed. She walked over to an empty bed and sat down.

"Aren´t you going to clean at all?" Complained one.

"Who me? I´m not a house cleaner. I´m here for the mission." They didn't say anything and just continued crying. She took a better look at them. They looked shaken to the core.

"So... What was with the harassment Kylen?" She asked carefully.

"That man said my boobs are fake!" Screamed the girl and burst out crying while another tried to calm her down. Jade looked at her obviously fake boobs and almost laughed, but covered her mouth soon enough.

"Oh my god! Look what you just did." Yelled the girl holding Kylen.

"Um... Whatever." She said and swung her hand.

"So who are you guys?"

"We are famous." Said Abby and blinked at her as if she was dumb.

"Of course. My bad. So you are?"

"I´m a star."

"Oh hell. Just tell me your name please." Jade almost shouted.

"My name is Khlo. I'm a social superstar."

"Cool. Where are you three from?"

"We are from Vigrior. We came here because it sounded like a spa place and then this man threw us in this cell. It´s all Abby´s fault!"

"Well, how could I know that stupid disc was evil?"

Jade stopped them "Hold up guys. You three found the disc by accident?"

"Aha." they nodded.

"And it was unlocked?"

"No my dad´s hacker unlocked it." Said Khlo.

"And you didn't see it said stuff about war?"

"Of course we did! This makeup brand was like... top!"

"Okaaaay..." This couldn't go on. These girls clearly, won´t last a day in the military. She had to find that creepy old man of theirs. She took Zmey from her pocket and sat him on her shoulder. She walked back to the round room. Her footsteps echoed in the empty hall behind her.

Wasteland

"Sir?" She called out.

"Go back to your room!" He shouted, but she couldn't see him.

"I´m looking for an old man!" She yelled back.

"I am the old man!" He replied.

"Okay, I need you then. There´s a huge problem!"

"What do you want now? I don't sell makeup!" She had to get his attention somehow.

"Can you show me a place where I can sharpen my knife?" He didn't answer, but she heard a loud thud behind her. She darted around and saw the guy had dropped down from the ceiling pipes.

"So obviously, you were lying, but what do you want?"

"I wasn't lying!" She pulled out the knife she stole from Andras.

"Look, man. I´ve been through some stuff and I ain't playing your games."

"Fair enough." He said and turned on his heels. She was not sure why the girls said he was an old man. He was about 25 years old. He was about one head taller than her. He had short brown hair in a messy hairstyle. He had a strong posture and tanned skin. He was wearing a black tank top and military pants. A blue anchor bracelet was gripping his wrist. She couldn´t see his face in detail, but she got curious.

"What´s with the beast?" he said jokingly almost playfully.

"Oh. That´s Zmey." Jade smiled.

"Well good luck keeping him alive on the battlefield."

"Can he come?" her eyes lit up.

"Sure. One cute soldier won´t do harm." She smiled and silently walked on. they entered a completely white room. It didn´t have windows or furniture. Just a few racks full of weapons.

"Whoa. What´s that?" She asked.

"Practice." He said and handed her a gun without turning around.

"Show me what you got."

"No thanks. I prefer knives." She said and walked over to the other rack. She found a special knife that split into two when you pulled it apart.

"Neat!" She said and threw it in her other hand in a way that made it spin in the air.

"Yeah. It´s my favorite." He walked to the middle of the room and yelled.

"Activate!" She could hear a machine start. A projector started projecting holograms across the room. Her knife´s blade disappeared and turned into blue particles.

"Good luck." Said the guy and loaded his gun.

Suddenly she could see a blue human, made completely of particles charging towards her with a huge machete. She leaned down as he swung and stabbed him in the back. The man collapsed, the particles dissolved and disappeared.

"Not bad." He said and Jade smiled. After a few seconds break a ton of other people appeared. The projector created a hologram of an old building. She hid behind a wall and waited to strike. A guy shot at her, but she dodged the bullet and it hit the other guy behind her. She stepped out of her cover and saw the army man fighting alongside her walking on holographic steps.

"Whoa! Technology is awesome!" He laughed and ran to the top. She ran after him and stood with her back against his.

"So what´s your name?" she asked.

"Rage! Yours?"

"Ja-!" The words stopped in her mouth. "I´m Envy." she turned around, and so did he. She stared into his eyes and noticed movement behind him. She threw her knife and it pierced the guy charging at them. She looked at his face again. She didn´t mind the holographs running around anymore. She was not sure if he looked beautiful or sinister. One of his eyes was dark brown. Almost black. The other one was blue, but it had a scar. The pupil was clearly cut open. His cheeks were slightly red. His lips were full, eyebrows bushy and lashes long. After the most awkward pause, she sighed.

"Woah."

Wasteland

"I knew it." He said and threw his gun at the floor.

"Knew what?"

"I knew you would hate the scar! Nobody can take me seriously as a general anymore!"

"I don't hate it!" She yelled, but he turned around. She stretched out her hand and moved her hair to the side.

"I´ve been to war too." She said.

"What happened?" He said, turned around, grabbed her hand and looked at her scars.

"Andras, mirrors, life."

"Sounds intense." He let go of her hand.

"It was, but I'm glad it happened. Don't let your scars define you. They represent courage and bravery."

"Thanks." He muffled and looked around the room. The holographic letters in the middle of the room said [GAME//OVER].

"That didn't go well..." He said and they both laughed.

In the evening, they were all sitting at the table. Rage, the three girls and her.

"So you three girls are going to war?" Asked Rage.

"No! We´re going famous!"

"Then you should leave. You can´t do that here." He sighed

"We are leaving when I say so!" yelled Abby.

"Girls! We are leaving this hellhole!" She announced. The girls stood up, flipped their hair, fixed their boobs and walked out.

"What was that all about?" Envy said and laughed.

"I don't have the heart to kill them like this." He said and bit into a piece of a meatloaf they got from a delivery truck earlier.

"So who are you?" She asked.

"Well, I've been in the military since I was six years old. My dad was a commander. Highly respected at the time. He went on a mission once and didn't come back. I decided to stay at the station.

My mom is still alive, but she hates the army. She divorced my dad right before the mission. She never visits me. I used to, but she just kept asking me when I'll have kids and marry so I gave up. Now I'm here to command the Hummingbird mission. You are great for it"

"Why so?" She raised her eyebrows.

"You are a great stealth killer."

"Ouch. That's harsh." She placed her cutlery on the plate and wiped her mouth. She was shocked that he knew her.

"Not really. Some things aren't meant to exist"

"Why?"

"We´ll talk another time. Good night Jade."

"Night." She said quietly and walked over to her room. It´s been a weird day she thought and petted Zmey behind his ears. He looked tired and hungry. Luckily, She still had some food left in her back-pack.

„Here you go." She smiled and offered him a handful of dried nuts. He took them all at once and settled down on her jacket in the corner of the room. She looked at the bag carelessly placed on the bunk bed.

"Well, that's it." She said to Zmey turned off the lights and laid down. She was tired and started drifting off to sleep. Slowly but peacefully. She felt protected like never before. This base was awesome! And suddenly there was nothing. No colors no feelings no thoughts. She wasn´t sure how it felt but it was calm. And after some time the sun rose above her head. She woke up. It was sunny and warm. She opened her eyes and the white light blinded her eyes. When they adjusted to the brightness, she saw a field. Green grass, flowers, and trees.

„It´s beautiful!" She exclaimed. She turned around and saw Dust holding North.

„Hey, guys!" She said and reached forward. Her eyes filled with tears of happiness and her chest felt like there was endless love all around. But then they turned around. They were crying black tears.

Wasteland

„You let us die!" They screamed in a demonic voice. It surprised her so she jumped back.

„Am I dead?" She asked carefully.

„No." She could hear a voice behind her. She turned around and saw Rage.

„it´s a simulation of your own thoughts. Not many people can do this."

"Why are you here with me?" She asked carefully.

"I saw something special in you and realized that you are just like me. Some call us mind projectors."

„And what do I do now?"

„Explore your mind."

„Okay." She said. Jade couldn't lie to herself. She was scared, petrified. She never liked her thoughts, but she stepped forward. On her left, there was a house. It was blue and white. Small but looked friendly.

„Go on." Said Rage. And she started taking steps towards the house. The soft grass was dancing beside her feet. The warm sun was shining on her face. She closed her eyes and kept walking on. Red light dimmed by the darkness of her eyelids dancing all around her it almost felt euphoric. But lucky as she was, she walked straight into the house fence and fell over in a horribly embarrassing scream. Before she even managed to get what happened she saw Rage laughing and rolling on the grass. She tried to look furious but burst out in loud laughter. They laughed for minutes.

„Sorry." She said with her eyes full of happy tears.

„It´s okay. I hadn't laughed like this in weeks," Said Rage. He gave her a hand standing up. She smiled and opened the house´s doors. The inside was painted red and there was blood on the floor. Her smile instantly disappeared and her stomach turned around. The smell was worse and it got chilly. She turned around to see Rage just as terrified. A loud thud disturbed the silence and echoed through the long hall.

„That was the door." Said Rage. Her mind spun for a bit as she realized what had just happened. She lost her ability to speak so she stood still. A cool breeze brought the whispers.

„We left because of you."

„What?!" She screamed and turned around to search the area.

„Who said that?" She called out. Rage looked worried and confused.

„Said what?" He asked. Then the whispers came again.

„It's us. Your dreams, wishes." Her head started to hurt but she fought back.

„Mom? Dad!" She screamed, but her voice was higher as usual.

„Jade no!" Jelled Rage.

„Don´t think! They aren´t real!" He said and held her hand tightly.

„You don't understand! They came back for me! I knew they would." She said with tears in her eyes.

„Don´t go!" Then it all went black and suddenly her head hit the floor. She looked around. She was in her old house where she grew up. It was in Eidhen. In Orbir. She lived here with her mom and dad back in the day. She stood up and everything seemed giant. She took a few steps forward and stopped in front of the door leading to the kitchen.

„Mom?!" She called out, but her voice was high. Surprised, she turned in the side to look in the mirror. Her eyes stopped on the carefully carved out wooden flowers and then her eyes meet the person in the mirror. It was a little girl. Her hair was short and brown. She had fair skin and freckles on her cheeks. Her short blue dress was carelessly flowing around her thighs. She looked confused and scared. She looked down at her tiny hands and started crying.

„Dad!" She screamed and ran the kitchen. She saw a woman. She was sitting at a table and typing something on a computer.

„Mom?" She said and tapped her on the shoulder.

„It´s me!" And tapped again. She didn't move a bit. Like she was frozen. It frustrated jade, so she grabbed her shirt and screamed.

„Hey!" At that moment, the woman stood up and looked at her

from above. Her eyes were black, her fingers were blue at the ends and her lips were cracked. jade got scared and tried to run away, but the woman grabbed her hand and looked at her straight in the eye. In the corner, she could see her dad. He looked like her mom. They both started walking towards her. Their voices mixed into a weird horrific tone.

„We never wanted you here. You are a mistake. Look! We have another child now. You meant nothing to anyone. No one knows where you came from. We took you home after we found you on the street. You were lying there and a letter was beside your head. We were so dumb to let you in our lives. Leaving you behind was the best thing we ever did!" And then the silence and blackness and the light. Her ears were ringing. She was in a white room. It looked like a simulator or something.

„Oh god, you finally woke up!" She could hear Rage.

„What happened?" She asked quietly.

„You manipulated your memories."

„I what?"

„Memory manipulation. The ability of hybrids."

„I´m a hybrid?"

„No, of course not. You just happen to be one of the people who had an old relative as one."

„Will you kill me?" She asked scared.

"No. That´s exactly why you are here." He answered carelessly.

„Okay. Why?"

„You´re special...well! We have a mission"

„what mission?" She asked curiously.

„To find that note your parents were talking about."

„Why!? I don't want to see that!" Jade yelled at him.

„You need to, so you can make peace with yourself."

„NO! I´m not going!"She screamed at him. Not minding her screaming and yelling he picked her up, put her over his shoulder and carried her resisting body to the car.

„Listen up! We're going, and you will cooperate! Please trust me."

„Okay, what about Zmey?"

„He´ll wait." Rage smiled.

„Fine." She mumbled and sat down. They set off and drove for hours. She didn't actually remember how long it took them. She fell asleep soon after they started driving

Wasteland

CHAPTER 17

The Hummingbird

CHAPTER 17: The Hummingbird

„Wake up sleepy-head" She felt Rage shaking her shoulder. She was wrapped up in a blanket. It was soft and warm.

„I want to wait here." She mumbled.

„You can't." She didn't mind the shaking and closed her eyes. The next thing she felt was cold mud on her face. The rain was sprinkling her hair and back. She looked up, confused and saw Rage laughing. She made a grumpy face at him and then let out a chuckle. She stood up and wiped her face.

"How did we get to Orbir in a day!?" She asked confused as hell.

"My little secret." He smiled at her.

„So where to?" She asked.

„Follow the memory." He said and stepped back. She turned to the black alley in front of her. She closed her eyes and an image appeared in front of her. She could see herself running down the street. She was small. About 5 years old.

„Wait!" She yelled and ran after her tiny self. The girl stopped at a blue building and opened the door. She tried to follow her inside but someone held her shoulder.

„You don't want to go in there. It´s just a memory." She nodded, shook her head and let her thoughts go. She opened her eyes and She was back, standing in front of the black alley.

"Follow me!" She said and smiled.

"That was a nice house you had."

"Wait what? You were there?"

"I told you Hybrid people can manipulate thoughts." He said winked and walked right past her staring face.

"Wait! So you are just like me?" She yelled and ran after him.

"Just like you." He nodded slightly.

"That´s so cool!"

"Really? Why?" He asked.

"Um... No idea." She said and laughed nervously and blushed

slightly.

"We´re here." Said rage and stopped in front of a blue worn down building with white wooden doors and windows. It felt familiar. Obviously.

"After you." Said Rage and looked towards the door. She slowly took a step forward and held the handle. It was cold and it sent shivers down her spine. The door creaked but didn't open. It was almost falling apart.

"I´m not sure about that Rage." She hesitantly turned back to him.

"Don't be a snowflake." He almost rolled his eyes.

"I know what will help." She said and stepped back.

"Please don't..."

"Watch me. And stop reading my mind!" She laughed and got ready. She inhaled and screamed as loud as possible.

"FRIED CAT!!" And she kicked the door open. They both laughed and the tension was gone. She entered the building and looked around. Her loud footsteps echoed through the halls. It was cold and worn down. There were broken chairs, tables, cabinets, and staircases. Her memories started to flow back into her mind.

"Control it." Said Rage behind her.

"I´ll do my best." She said unsure.

"I know where the note is. There´s a room I used to stay in, but it´s upstairs."

"No worries. I got it." Said Rage and stood in front of the broken staircase. He took a rope from his backpack and swung it over the fence that looked stable enough.

"Ladies first." He said and handed her the rope. She wrapped it around her hand and leaned on the wall with her legs. She walked up with ease.

"You´re a real ninja woman." Said Rage, following her up.

"Arvas would be proud" She laughed back and slowly took some steps towards her old room. She saw Rage´s face go pale when she mentioned Arvas. He must have known him...

Wasteland

"I remember this place." She said quietly. When she walked into the room, she saw a big window in front of her. It was wide open and the curtains were waving in the cold wind blowing from the outside. The wallpaper was peeling and the floor was scratched. There was a bunk bed in the corner and a playing corner under it. A dark blue rug was covering the floor in the middle and there was a large Drawer on her left.

"If it isn´t in there it´s gone." She said and opened the drawer. There were some clothes in it. She swiped them away and held up a letter. She took a closer look. It was old and a bit torn. Her hand was shaking.

"Well. Go on." Said Rage. She opened it and started reading out loud.

"If you are reading this, your life will now change forever. Sorry about the confusion, but you´ve been chosen already. Your mission was to take care of this person until at least five years old and then leave it alone for us to transfer it to one of our bases."

"Why am I called an >it<."?

"Because by the army you are always considered a subject. The army captured you and transmitted you to another family."

"But why?"

"Because you´re something extraordinary. You have the ability to develop supernatural powers." She took another paper from the letter.

"Hello, baby. We love you! Remember that. Although they will take you away in a few minutes. I know it doesn't seem fair, but I also know you can save all of us." She remained silent for a few moments and then spoke.

"They just let me go."

"They had to, or else the warriors would kill you."

"If I belonged to the military...How did Arvas get me then?"

"Arvas is an old friend of mine. He chose to protect the abducted children and trained them to protect themselves." She just nodded.

Jade took the last paper out and unfolded it. A few photos fell to the ground. She carefully picked them up and swapped trough them. There was her, smiling at her foster parents, them swimming, walking in the park. Her eyes watered. She sat down and hugged her knees tightly.

"It´ll be okay." She heard Rage´s voice behind her. He placed his hand on her back and she darted around and threw herself in his arms. She tightly hugged him and cried.

"I´m sorry." She managed to squeeze out of herself.

"It´s okay. I got you." He replied calmly and placed his hand on her head. She felt like a little kid.

She couldn´t possibly know how long they sat there, but when she calmed down, she was hungry as hell. She used Rage´s shoulder to stand up and smiled slightly.

"Ahoy pirate! Where to now?"

"Back to the base. We got a warning call." Replied Rage.

"Why didn't we leave immediately?!"

"Because you needed some time."

"How do you plan to drive there that quickly?"

"I don't." He said and pulled out a small stone.

"Here we go!" He grabbed her hand and she grabbed the letter. Suddenly there was darkness all around her. She could walk to the right, left or any way she wanted, but she never moved. She completely lost track of time and space.

"Hello?" She yelled out. Rage answered.

"Ah, good." Then in a second, a white beam of light spread through the darkness. She looked around her. She was standing in the hallway of the base. The walls were spinning around her, so she closed her eyes. When she opened them again, she could see Rage above her head.

"Hello, sleepyhead!" He shouted. She screamed in fear and darted up.

"What the hell is wrong with you? You scared me!" She yelled and then they both started laughing.

"So what was that?" She asked curiously.

"That's my second Hybrid power." Her jaw dropped to the floor and he proceeded to explain.

"My grandpa was a Hybrid. Therefore, the genes are still close to me. He had the power of teleportation. I can only use it while I have a special stone with me. It´s extremely energy draining. Anyway, my grandpa was executed for being >illegal<

"I´m sorry about your grandpa," she said carefully.

"It´s okay..." He said and smiled at the stone.

"So...What was so urgent?" She asked in excitement.

"They are deploying us early. In two hours. Get packing."

"Wait... For the mission?"

„Yes. Don't be scared! I'll give you the equipment."

„Okay." She mumbled trying to sound Brave. Rage walked down a narrow staircase to a glass door.

„Ladies first," He said and held the door open. She walked through and there were mannequins in Black outfits.

„Put it on," He said.

„What? That one?" She asked, and pointed across the room.

„No. That one." He said. Rage held her arm and dragged it to the right until it stopped on a different mannequin. She walked over and felt the material. It was heavy on her fingers. It was grey and black.

„Put it on." Rage repeated himself in a calm tone.

„Mmmmm... Could you turn around for a second?"

„Sure thing." He laughed and spun around on his heels. She dropped her clothes on the floor and yelled over her shoulder.

„Don´t peek!"

„I won't, don't worry." First, she put on black pants. They looked like his with tons of pockets, zippers and a chain to hold different weapons. They were tight but wrinkled. The best words to describe them was badass. The next piece of clothing was a shirt. It was grey with a black pattern scattered across the shoulders. There were triangles and squares. It was made of a light sporty fabric. She pulled it on as fast as possible and grabbed the chest plate. It was made of several black matte painted steel plates to form an artistic looking shape. It reminded her of Osen´s. she pulled it on and it snapped together on her back with a magnet. It covered one of her shoulders and the opposite hip. It was quite heavy. Then she grabbed the shoes. They were just normal black military styled shoes. But the final thing was the gloves. One went up to the elbow and was covered with the same metal plates as the chest plate. It looked like a tiny shield. The other one was short. Just large enough to cover her palm and wrist. Both gloves were cut on the other side, so they only covered half of the fingers. They were completely black with zippers on the other side.

„Whoa! You look so cool!" She heard Rage from the other side of the room.

„You promised not to look!" She yelled sarcastically and started laughing. She continued to talk.

„So where can I see myself?"

„Huh? Oh yeah sure. Come with me!" She followed him to a black room. He stopped in the middle and held her shoulders. He moved her a little bit to the left and a bit forward.

„There! Stay!" He walked out and stood by the door.

„Ready?"

„I guess." She said and he turned on the lights. The outfit looked stunning. It fit her perfectly.

„How does it fit so-"

„Laser measurements."

„And when did you-"

„When you walked in."

„Did I let you-?"

„Nope, and no. I don't care."

Wasteland

„Do I look okay or do I-"

„You look stunning."

„Ow... Thanks." She said, smiled and blushed a little.

„Next room!" Rage yelled and pulled her by the hand. The next moment she was sitting behind a holographic computer.

[COSTUMISE YOUR STYLE]

„Oh cool. Like in a video game?" She asked and looked over to Rage. He nodded.

„You have to change at least one feature. We can` t let Osen know who you are." His face was dead serious. He walked out and she started clicking.

[EYE COLOR]

„No..."

[PASTIC SURGERY]

„Nope."

[HAIRSTYLES]

„Yep! That´s the one." she picked her style.

[LONG]

[BEACH WAWES]

[SILVER-WHITE]

„Let´s hope for the best." She crossed her fingers.

[ACCEPT]

She sat still for about 5 minutes until the display announced.

[APPLICATION COMPLETE]

Jade stood up from the chair and walked over to the large mirror on the wall.

„Whoa." She was speechless she looked so different and certainly more mature. It looked kind of hot though. She thought.

„Sure it does." Says Rage and laughed at her.

„Can you stop reading my mind? It's creeping me out." She said and smiled. He walked over to her.

„We can leave now. I packed your gear. Are you ready?"

„Ready as I'll ever be." She said in a sad tone. She followed him through a hallway.

"The plane is leaving in ten minutes from the top of the roof. We have to get there in five." He pressed a button and a glass door of the elevator opened.

"What about Zmey?" Envy asked sadly.

"Don´t worry. I got that covered. He´s coming. Just don't mention him ok?"

"Okay. Thank you." She whispered softly.

They stood next to each other. She took a better look a Rage´s outfit. His pants and the shirt were the same as hers, but the chest plate was covering both of his shoulders. Both of his gloves were long. The outfit felt really comfortable for a steel piece of clothing. The most noticeable thing on his outfit was a mask covering a part of his face. It was obviously there to cover his scarred eye. She was curious about what happened to him. But she stopped herself. After all, he could read minds. She nervously took a glance at him.

"It´s a long story. I´ll tell you some other day. And don't be nervous around me. We´re friends." She shivered but forced a smile.

"Sorry Rage." She mumbled and cleared her mind. The elevator ride felt like it lasted forever. They finally stepped on the roof and she started getting a bad feeling in her stomach.

"Are you with me? It´s now or never." Rage said and offered her his hand. She was a bit shaken up, but she tried to stay calm. She grabbed his hand tightly.

"Let's do this!" She nodded.

"Calm down." He said to her.

"I´ll be okay." She replied. He gripped her hand tighter. He looked just as scared. If Osen ever found out they will all be hanging.

"We´re in this together."

They stepped inside the plane and locked themselves on the chairs.

Wasteland

It was rather large painted in futuristic colors. The chairs were spacious and rather comfortable compared to what she was used to. She couldn´t remember much of the trip. There were no windows. She tried asking about the mission, but nobody knew for sure what was going on.

CHAPTER 18

Hopeless War

CHAPTER 18: Hopeless War

The ringing in her ears was now slowly wearing off. The plane was loud as hell. She was now sitting in a damaged building with ten other people about her age...they were all over 20 years old though. She was playing with the necklace she took from that jewelry stand.

"How are you feeling?" Asked commander Maple. He was in charge of the hummingbird mission. His skin was dark and he had a wide chiseled body. He looked strong and sturdy. Like any war general. The only really special thing about him was the dirty blonde hair put in a man bun.

"I'm fine, thanks" She replied, trying not to look scared. Maple continued his speech.

"So! We are located in sector 13. The main power generator is south in sector 4." He pointed towards the middle of the map lying on the ground.

"If we manage to break in and unplug the data and disconnect the wired network all the technology should disappear and Osen will be left without it. This could buy all the rebels across the 3 worlds time to resist. If that doesn't work we will blow the main generator up. That would do the same." A woman across the room stood up.

„Why don't we blow it up as plan A?"

„Because if we do, you won´t ever get back home. "

„Ow." She sighed.

„NOW!" Maple clapped once to catch our attention.

„Get some sleep. Tomorrow we are moving to sector seven. Good night."

„Good night." They all replied, turned off the flashlights and covered themselves with sleeping bags. Envy´s mind wouldn't stop racing all over the place. Suddenly her thoughts stopped. All she could see in her head was Dust holding North. Their grey and blue eyes, blond and white hair and North´s tiny hands. A tear escaped her eye.

„Brothers?" Asked Rage who was lying next to her.

„No... Very dear friends." She said trying not to sound hurt.

„It´s okay." Rage put his hand on her shoulder. It was warm and it calmed her down.

„Thank you." She said in tears and gripped his arm. She fell asleep still holding on to it.

„Get up!" Yelled Maple. The whole group opened their eyes still half asleep. Maple proceded to talk.

„Now let's move!" He yelled. They all got up without saying a word, grabbed their backpacks and started walking. Nobody was talking and then she suddenly heard Rage scream. She turned around to look around in terror and saw him walking beside her completely normally. You're going crazy she thought to herself. She was confused because she could hear him but he wasn´t talking. Like she could read his thoughts...

„Yay good job. You made it." She heard Rage.

„That´s quite amazing." She answered with her thoughts.

„But is there any way to hide my thoughts?"

„Sure it is. Just put on this ring." He silently handed her a black ring with red stones. She slipped it on her finger and he went quiet. She pulled it off again.

„This will disable all hybrid powers surrounding you. Including your own. Use it wisely." She put the ring on and looked at him. He winked at her and smiled. She smiled back and they continued walking.

They walked for a few hours. Her legs were tired and she was starving.

„Stop!" Yelled commander Maple.

„We will stop here in front of sector 7. It requires stealth to pass. We will need Asher and Joyce to clear it."

„Yes sir!" a girl and a guy stepped forward.

Wasteland

„Do your work." Said Maple.

„Yes, sir!" They yelled in unison and ran off towards the large black border wall.

„Will they make it?" She turned to Rage.

„Let´s hope so." He sighed and opened his backpack.

„But how can Maple send them out like that?"

„They are the only ones who have their invisibility power trained."

„But that's a sacrifice."

„They are trying here to save thousands."

„So selfless. I wish I was more like them." She sighed and looked down at her feet.

„But you are." Said Rage.

„You came here to fight for others. That's hella brave!" She sat down and thought for a bit.

„But I had nothing."

„Like everyone else here. They wouldn't choose people with big differences. You see, everyone here grew up without parents. Everyone here was hurt, had challenges. And..."

„And?"

„And not many people care about us. So the loss wouldn't hurt as much." Her eyes watered but she didn't cry. It was the harsh truth.

„Oh...I understand. I'm sorry."

„it´s okay." He said and picked up her hand. He pulled her towards him and shoved her hand into his backpack. She gasped in fear when she felt a furry warm ball in it, but she suddenly realized what it was and smiled wide to her ears.

„Zmey." She whispered.

„Hi, little buddy." She petted the little ball.

„How did you manage to get him in?" She looked at Maple.

„Well Maple said I could, but he can't touch the ground. It's full of sharp rocks that could give him an acid infection."

„Ow." She said and looked down the backpack.

„Good luck buddy." She said and petted him again.

„Settle down. We're moving on tomorrow." Said Maple in a harsh tone.

„Sector 7 is the outer inhabited sector. That means we have to fight. You have to get your weapons ready but the main tactic is stealth. That's why we are a small group. We won't survive a fight with over 50 soldiers, so be as quiet as possible. You also have to watch out for warriors. The 5th sector is flooded with them. We don't know what's waiting behind these gates. Now get some rest." Maple sat down and took a bite out of a big sandwich. Jade´s stomach growled so she unzipped her backpack. There was a bottle of water and some kind of weird meat.

„It´s good." She heard Rage next to her.

„You tried that?" She asked in disgust and almost gagged.

„Mhm!" She turned around and saw Rage with his mouth stuffed with food. She started laughing at the sight of his chubby cheeks.

„sfop lauhin! I´m fonna sfit it ouf!" He tried to mumble, but it looked so hilarious she only started laughing even louder. In 10 seconds, they were both laughing together on the floor, trying to calm down. War is brutal, but they had to hold on to any little ray of happiness they could find.

„Want to go for a walk?" He asked when they calmed down.

„Sure why not." She smiled. They took Zmey out of the backpack and Jade put him on her shoulder. The little guy licked his hind leg and made a clicking sound. They started walking towards some broken-down buildings in the distance.

„It´s weird to see the other side of war is also suffering." She sighed.

„We can win this, right?" She asked carefully.

„Nobody wins in war. It's a total waste of time and lives." They sat down on a big concrete block from a destroyed building above them. It was grey with yellow typing all over it. They hadn't seen any green plants all the time spent there. It was quite depressing to think about it. The world was despite everything still dark and wasted.

Wasteland

„Can I ask you something?" she spat out.

„Ah. You want to know about her scar." She felt her cheeks get hot red.

„Yeah…That." She said.

„I was still little. My parents and I lived in a small field house on a meadow in the middle of the forest. It was old, and a bit falling apart but we made it work. I had a little sister. We´d always play in the attic. One day we were playing with wooden swords we made in the woods the other day. The play got a bit heated and I launched towards her. She was one year younger than I was. I accidentally pushed her through the large glass window. She fell about 10 meters from the house. I tried to stop and save her. I really did, but I couldn't. I failed. She fell and a big glass shard pierced through her body. I killed a 4-year-old. I can still hear her scream spilling over the green hills. My mom ran to her immediately, but we lived too far away from the hospital to help her. My parents didn´t talk to me for 2 months after the incident. They hated me. They still do. I have a few scars on my hand from it. And the Ugly one on my eye."

„Why do you still blame yourself? You were just kids. Accidents happen." Jade looked into his eyes.

„I can't not. I killed my own sister." His eyes were watery from the tears.

„It was an accident. And your scars aren´t ugly."

„Well never mind." He shook his head and wiped the tears with his hand.

„No. Go face your fears. I did it too." Envy said and looked him in the eyes with determination.

„There is no way I can face her! I'll just throw up." Said Rage.

„I can help you." She offered.

„We can do this together." She put her hand over his and watched him close his eyes. She shut her eyes too, and in a few moments, she could see sunlight, a field and a small blue house in the middle.

CHAPTER 18: Hopeless War

CHAPTER 19

Sector 4

Rage was standing to her left. She could feel he was scared to death.

"Calm down." She said gently and let go of his hand.

"It´ll be okay." She smiled and gazed across the field. She took a few small steps towards the small blue house. A small path was leading to it. Rage stopped suddenly.

"I can´t." He cried out.

"You have to let this go." She said and pulled him inside. The door slammed shut behind them. Rage silently started walking towards the attic. When they reached it, he was a five-year-old with a wooden sword and a paper hat on his head. Jade remained silent when they heard a tiny scream behind them.

"Amy let´s play!" Little rage ran to the attic with a 4-year-old girl.

"Wait for me sky!" she yelled back at him. Sky? Why would he change his name to Rage? Time stopped and Rage started taking steps towards the playful Sky. With every step he took, the time forwarded a bit. With every step he took, Sky was slowly pushing Amy through the huge glass pane. The sounds and laughter echoed in Jade´s ears. When rage reached Sky, Amy was already leaning through the window. Rage stepped directly into the boy and reached for her stretched out hand. The time stopped completely. Pieces of glass were scattered all over the air. Jade could hear Amy screaming and Rage talking to her.

"Amy you will be okay." His fingers were touching hers. His voice was cracking as he spoke. He was almost crying.

"Let go." She silently walked over and held his shoulders.

"It wasn´t your fault."

"I´m so sorry Amy." He cried out and suddenly, the pieces of glass blasted into the air cutting her lip. She held her hand over the bleeding cut and shut her eyes. The air was filled with colorful shattered glass particles spinning and shining in the sunlight. Rage collapsed, his head buried in his palms. He was now back to being his normal, older self. She slowly walked over to him.

"Your sister isn´t mad at you." Said jade gently. "She never was. Don´t worry."

Amy´s screaming was slowly dying in the background. The next thing Jade could see was Rage on his knees, sobbing. She kneeled down and put her hand on his back.

"Don´t look at me!" He yelled at her.

"Why... What´s wrong." She said carefully.

"I´m a monster!" He showed her away.

"That´s the most ridiculous thing I've ever heard." She resisted and gripped his arm. She could see the surroundings slowly fading away.

"Do you have a tissue?" He asked, sitting on a rock beside her. His eye was bleeding. Jade silently handed him a tissue and they stood up silently, scared to disturb the dead silence around them.

"Don´t tell anyone." He warned her. Envy crossed her chest with her index finger.

"You have my word."

She lifted Zmey on her shoulder and they started walking back to the camp. The sky had turned black and the cold air was hurting her nose as she inhaled. Rage treasured how young and innocent Envy was despite all the killing she endured. Her eyes were sparkling with hope. The fire was half burnt out when they arrived at the camp. Maple and the others were sitting around it in a circle and talking about future mission plans. They listened to Maple talk. Nobody questioned where they were as they silently rejoined the group.

„So when we destroy the power generator everything will return to centuries back." He explained.

„No cars, no computers no electricity. And it will be impossible to provide it from anything else. The sun is dimmed already, the wind is too strong and the world ran out of coal."

Everyone else was quiet and didn't dare to speak. They knew what it meant if they destroyed the generator. They were risking the catastrophe of all 3 lands. Rage held his head. Why did he come

Wasteland

here? It was hopeless anyway. There was no point in fighting.
Jade was sleeping beside him. She reminded him of his wife. He
wanted her back so much. Why did they get into that stupid fight?
Why did it have to be right when the army marched in. He almost
sobbed. Fighting tears he closed his eyes and slowly fell asleep. He
missed her and wondered if she was still alive and prayed to himself
that she was alright. He would accept anything just to make sure she
was ok. For a brief moment, he hoped she had found another man
to protect her.

Before she realized, Jade was walking into sector 7. The huge
concrete walls were brooding on the sky like giants always carefully looking down on them. The group sneaked past hundreds of
soldiers. They jumped roofs, climbed walls and stopped in front of
sector 5. Maple started talking. Quietly, but powerful.

„We will enter the armed part. Be prepared." They all stood quiet
for a while and Maple continued. You could taste the fear lurking
in the air around them.

„One person will have to go with me to unplug the generator." He
raised his eyebrows.

„Any volunteers?" Nobody dared to say a word.

„Thought so. I will pick one of you." He said and scattered tiny
withe papers across the dirty ground.

„Each of these papers has a name on it. Good luck." He circled
above the ground with his hand and picked a paper on the top left.
He nervously licked his lips And unwrapped the crumbled note.

„Envy." He called out.

Jade's head spun and her heart dropped.

„There is a chance you won't come home again. Be prepared." He
said and patted her on the shoulder roughly. No. This couldn't be
happening. She couldn't just die like this. But the game was fair.
She chose to come here. She had to do it. It was a draw.

„We leave in an hour!" Yelled maple from the background. The
sudden warmth on her shoulder surprised her. It was Rage. He
hugged her tight from the back. She clenched her teeth and gripped

his arms. Her heart jumped at the thought of being with him. He was really special. Different but still exactly like her. In the past week since they met they bonded so much that she could recognize him anywhere. It almost felt like love. Her stomach was a tight knot and she thought of Dust. Thank god she had her power ring on. What would Rage think about her thoughts? Could he possibly feel something towards too? She shook her head.

„I can't let you die like this." He said with a soft voice. She shook her head.

„I wouldn't change anything about my life. It was all worth it."

„Don't talk like this!" He snapped at her. „I won't let you die." He pressed his cheek against hers. She could feel a small tear slipping from his eye running down his warm face.

„Knock, knock," He said, sounding hurt.

„Who´s there?" She asked reluctantly

„Envy."

„Envy who?"

„Envy you because you´re amazing." He smiled weakly at her.

They spent the hour laughing on the ground. It was a desperate attempt to kill the sadness slowly crawling over everyone's faces.

„Line up. Leave the guns at the door. They are all-electric and will blow up near the generator." His commands were muffled in the background

„Come on! Go forward! March through the gates! It's open! Run!" Jade forced her legs to run and they slipped through a small gap in the wall.

„We're in." Maple exhaled in a calm tone. A loud echoing noise was filling the round-shaped 4th sector. Maple pulled out a map. He started pointing at random locations. Everything felt like a hazy blur happening in the background. All she could focus on was her heavy breathing and her boots hitting the hard ground.

„The generator is west from here. You will move around numbers 3, 6 and 7 to cover all the passages. I and Rage will try to disable the generator."

Envy's heart dropped.

„Rage!?" She saw him slowly walk towards maple. The world was running in slow motion.

„Why." She squeezed out half crying. He glanced at her and signed >I'm sorry< with his lips and started running behind Maple. Every step he took sliced through her heart. Betrayal was echoing in her head. She felt dizzy. A woman was shouting at her. She only picked up a few words.

„Focus...sector 4...army...defend...Rage."

„Rage!?" Her mind was suddenly clear.

„Yes, I understand! Position 6, defend the generator." Jade spit out and shook her head.

„Good." Said the woman and tapped her on the shoulder. „Follow me." They ran across a small black bridge placed above an insanely deep hole in the ground.

„Incoming!" Yelled the woman as they saw a few soldiers running towards them.

CHAPTER 20

Staying Alive

CHAPTER 20: Staying alive

The guy who was with them attacked with his double swords and 2 dropped dead in painful screams. Jade got her knife ready and gripped it tightly. She never knew how to shoot a gun. Arvas knew it was useless, way before anyone else did. Her hand was shaking as she charged ahead. Her fingers gripped the handle tighter as she jumped to the fence and swiftly made her way behind a man. She launched the knife at his back making him fall face front on the floor. She pulled it out just as quickly and threw it straight in the other man's chest. Adrenaline had completely taken over her body. Jade felt strong and powerful. Like at the time when she finished training with Arvas. Nothing could stop her now. She looked and acted like an animal determined to hunt her prey. That was the trait she learned while Arvas trained her. She was made to be a killing machine, an invisible hunter that could kill without being seen. She would never let the soldiers get to Rage. She had to stop them no matter the price. Her thoughts kept going out of focus. The woman was yelling something from a hole deep in the ground. She fell. Jade took a moment to look down and almost threw up. The woman´s leg bones were twisted weirdly, piercing through her stomach and spilling parts of her on the ground below. The man was now laying on the ground far from her. And Envy kept fighting. It was clear that the mission was hopeless in terms of returning home. One man here one there. She missed Dust. She missed his eyes, his blonde hair. She loved him, though she never admitted it. And now it was too late. It was too late for her to live. She couldn't imagine never being able to hold his hand again. It's been more than a year since she last saw him. Her breath was getting short and her hands were tired. **KEEP FIGHTING** her brain commanded her, but she collapsed with the image of Dust before her eyes. She was vunerable.

„I can't." She sighed. The cold wall was sending chills down her spine. She breathed loudly and grunted as she pulled herself against a nearby wall. She took her backpack and unzipped it. Zmey was shaking in fear. She took him out and put him in her lap. She offered hem a few dried nuts from her pocket. He made her feel not so lonely. She was sitting hidden in a corner, surrounded by metal parts and wires.

„You know Zmey. I think my life was pretty okay." She slowly took a sip from her water bottle. Her face was sweaty and had a few small cuts.

„I achieved some positive stuff, right? I tried to take care of North

He was a great kid. Way too young to die. I got rid of a few bastards. I got a pet. I reunited with an old friend. I found out my parents didn't really hate me. I hope they could be proud of my life for just a minute. Hell, a second if. I wish I could see them again, but they are probably dead. Like everyone else, I had ever loved. I wonder if I had any brothers and sisters. I even managed to fall in love in my whole life. I wish I could hug him again before I leave." A tear dropped from her eye at the thought of her long lost friend from the mines.

„I tried to fight. I did my best to save the world from the dark lord. Oh, Zmey if you knew... You don't understand what's going on, you don't know we will both be gone soon. You just enjoy every moment you are given. I wish I could be like you." She petted the confused animal on its head. And it laid down on her chest. She could hear a person walking around the corner. That was it. She would die on the spot. She had no choice. She wanted to scream, but she couldn't. She wanted to run, but her legs failed. She closed her eyes and hugged Zmey tightly. She was crying. Helpless. She opened her eyes and a soldier was standing in front of her. She could feel his grin under the black gas mask. There was so much hatred under that mask she couldn´t even begin to comprehend it.

Suddenly, the whole sector went silent. The confused soldier ran away towards the Generator. That gave Jade the energy to launch herself up.

„They did it!" She yelled lifting her fists high in the air.

„They disabled it!" She ran towards the generator. The whole sector was falling down. She ran across the whole battlefield, stepping over lifeless bodies like they were logs on a grass path. It was horrible to look at it, but it was war in its whole bliss. The battlefield was silent. She made her way to the middle, where the generator was located.

„Maple!" She screamed at a black figure running towards her.

„We did it!" She smiled „We won!"

„Gas! Run!" Yelled maple gasping for air.

„What?!" Envy was confused and stopped running.

„The gas is poisonous!" He yelled when he passed her. „Stay low!" He added. His skin was covered in horrible white blisters.

Rage wasn't outside. She glanced at the building. And her heart pounded. There was dark smoke coming from it. Gas masks couldn't stop it judging from the suffocating enemy soldiers around it. She took the mask off and ripped apart her shirt. She covered her mouth with it and ran into the room full of smoke.

„Rage!" She yelled. Her skin and eyes were already burning in excruciating pain.

„Damn it! Where are you?" This time it was more desperate. She kicked open all the doors and finally found him lying motionless on the ground.

„Rage you have to stand up." She yelled and her head started spinning. She felt like throwing up. Without thinking, she dropped the fabric, grabbed his leg and started pulling him out. She took a deep breath and it felt like her lungs were falling apart from the acid. She started coughing and choking.

„Are you dumb?" Said Rage half crying in pain.

„Run. There's no chance for me." His voice was trembling.

„We are getting out of this together." She managed to say and kept pushing herself forward. The gas made her want to stop and die, but she had the chance to do something right for once. She could have something to be proud of. She took the last big heath and pulled again. She was almost there. The room was spinning around her. What if she didn't make it. No. She couldn't lose another friend. It was enough. Her muscles tensed and she pushed herself outside. She fell down the stairs and breathed. Next to her, there was lying Rage. His face was pale and blood was coming from his mouth. She failed. He didn't make it. No. Not again. Not like this. The thoughts hurt her head. The world became black. She couldn't move or talk. She could barely hear and see. She failed. Again. Everything was lost. She stared at Rage´s bleeding face and place her dirty hand on his cheek.

„Sorry...“

A servant entered the dark lord's chambers back in Ijos. He stopped before Osen, sitting on a throne and bowed to the floor.

„Best sir. They destroyed the main generator.“

„Good.“ Osen grinned. „Did you burn cars, ships, and planes?“

„Most of them your majesty.“ Osen laughed.

„We are returning to the most powerful era of Dowak. I shall build my kingdom on the ashes of this world.“ He signed the servant to leave and sat back on his throne. He was close to completing his plans. And even the rebels were working for him. Sure, destroying the generator caused more damage than good at the moment, but just like him, the rebels were out of technology as well. He was now able to restore the world from the old Wisgard legacy. To build it again. Stronger, even more advanced. The servant closed the large door of the mansion leaning towards the red sky. Little did everyone know what the dark lord's plans really were.

CHAPTER 21

A Bitter Victory

CHAPTER 21: A Bitter Victory

Envy woke up in a bright building. The sun was shining through the glass on the ceiling. It looked a lot like a hospital. She was alone in the room, lying on a white bed, covered with a white blanket. A tube was leading from her hand to a bottle of a clear liquid. Some people were talking outside the room. She couldn't make out what they were saying. Her head was spinning and her vision was corrupted with black spots. She passed out again. She woke up to the sound of loud footsteps running along the hallway outside.

„We've been attacked!" A woman's voice was screaming. That can't be good. Jade stood up and looked around the room. There were no weapons. Of course. It was a hospital. She couldn't run. She was dressed in a long light white tunic and had no pants. She just sat down, helpless and waited for the attack to pass. After an hour, the hospital went silent. She quietly sat up on the bed and looked around. The room was spacious with a huge glass window facing the wasteland of dust outside. This couldn´t have been Ixah. She looked down at her arms and finally noticed it. Her whole right hand was missing up to the elbow and has been replaced with a steel, mechanical one. She sighed but felt relieved to be alive. She slowly moved the fingers on her new arms and gripped them into a fist. The room was completely white and sterile. she stretched her arms and violently pulled the tubes attached to her out of her arm. Her bare feet touched the cold floor and she walked around the room and towards the exit.

She opened the glass door, stepped out in the hallway, and looked around. There were windows on each room, visible only from the outside. She walked along the hall and checked every window. Some rooms were empty. Some had people sleeping in them and then she noticed it. There was Rage. Her heart skipped a beat when she realized he was doing okay and she smiled wide. She carefully approached the door and it slid open with ease. He was holding a baby girl in his arms. Was he crying? She blinked twice and shook her head. How was this possible? She saw him die. This couldn't have been real. She stepped into the room.

„Rage?" She said aloud.

„Shhhhhh." He covered his mouth with a finger and started whispering. „She's asleep." She whispered too.

„Who is this?"

„I never told you, but I had a wife. We got in a fight and I applied to the mission." Jade smiled slowly. Her heart was a little broken at the thought she couldn´t be with Rage but she was happy.

„This is her." Said Rage and stroked a sleeping woman's brown hair. „And this is my lovely daughter." He smiled and looked back at the baby.

„I'm so happy for you Rage." Said Jade. And she was. She wanted to yell. She wanted to sing. She had saved a family! The baby started crying and the woman next to them woke up. She took the baby and looked at Envy with a confused look.

„Who is this Sky?" She asked.

„This is Jade." He glanced at her. „She saved my life on the battlefield." The woman started shaking. She stood up. She was almost crying now. She threw her arms around Jade and started thanking her. She was crying. It made her feel awkward but Jade saw she was happy.

„It's okay." She said and smiled. The woman sat back down and Rage turned to Jade again.

„Listen to me. You can't stay here." He held her arms still. „They know who you are and they don't like it. Run as far as you can. They may be rebels, but they don't trust anyone who trained with Arvas."

She sighed, „I don't blame them. We were trained to become killing machines."

„Good luck Jade. If you need me, just find me. I'll be here to help." She nodded but her heart denied. She didn't need any help. She was a warrior. She was strong. Sky held open his arms and she hugged him tightly.

"Thank you for everything." She said, happily.

Wasteland

"No. Thank YOU." He looked her in the eyes and heard him speak in her head. "I owe you for the rest of my life. You´re a good person. Don´t beat yourself up."

She nodded thankfully and walked out.

Zmey quickly jumped on her shoulder and just like that, she ran off. She ran outside. Everything connected to technology was gone. All the cars, all the machines. And the world looked duller than ever before. But they had won. They destroyed the generator. Osen will need some time to gain his strength again. They had to strike as soon as possible. They could defeat him once and for all. She could defeat him once and for all. She had the chance. All she had to do was find him and slit his neck. But who was she lying to? She was weak. She only had a white tunic and a gas mask. She stood no chance against his army.

After a week out alone she found some clothes. They weren‘t the best, but they protected her feet and body from the burning hot dust. After 2 more weeks, she was almost too weak to walk. She was hungry, she was tired. Her whole body was aching. Her head was spinning all the time. Could she be sick? No. That wasn‘t possible. She had to find a way to Weyn. She had to reach Eliard. It wasn‘t that far. It couldn‘t be. Yes. She will find it. She will defeat Osen. She will win this war. She will put an end to suffering. She. Arvas‘s warrior. She was trained for it. She was trained to win. The wind was playing with her white-silver hair and a loose black T-shirt. She was close. Almost there.

CHAPTER 22

Twisted Reality

CHAPTER 22: Twisted Reality

She had read about Weyn in a book. It was called Weyn-powers. It was a book about hybrids. It said that they all lived in a protected land in the north called Weyn. They had locked themselves away. They saw the future. Osen would kill them all. They protected themselves. The legend said it was a world from another dimension you had to pass the magic gates to get to it. Only people with magic powers were allowed to enter it freely. But she could do it. She had to. They could teach her the powers she could develop. She could use them to fight. To win! The magic gate was the closest to Eliard. Anglers' town in north Orbir. She could swim to it. It was so close. It took her weeks to come there.

She sneaked on Osen's ships. She had come so far, only to find the sea. An endless ocean of grey, muddy water was all around her.

She collapsed in disappointment. It had to be there. It was on the map. She threw the book it the ocean and screamed. It wasn't fair. With these powers, she could do wonders. She sighed and closed her eyes. She was dumb to believe in some magical powers anyway. It was evening and she was tired. The sand from the beach was warming her body. She fell asleep.

She had to be dreaming. She was standing on the beach, but it was clean. The water was clear blue and the sun was bright yellow. She was wearing her white tunic again. The water was calling her and she listened. Someone was singing. It was a beautifully sad song about pain and destruction. Jade stepped into the cold refreshing water. The waves were splashing around her ankles and playing with her legs. She went deeper and deeper. In the distance, there was a silhouette of land. She kept her eyes on it and kept sinking deeper. The water was now touching her hips, but she kept going. Somehow, she just knew she had to. The water rose to her shoulders and chin. Suddenly, the ground disappeared and something pulled her under the water. She panicked and resisted, but she kept sinking lower in the ocean. She looked around and saw the ocean people. A beautiful female was dragging her lower into the ocean. Her eyes were bright yellow. She had long green hair and gills covering her neck. Instead of legs, she had a big grey fishtail. Her breasts were covered in fish skin that slowly dissolved into human skin on her neck, stomach, and back. Her hair and face were covered in shiny seashells and pearls. Jade was running out of air and snapped out of her magical state. She had no other choice, but to breathe in. Water filled her lungs and piercing pain flew through her chest. Her vision was dark and blurry. She slowly lost her consciousness, but she still heard the singing. She was alone, in the dark water. She had gone crazy. This time for sure. It was beautiful. She didn't understand the language but she knew what they were saying. She felt how they pulled her out of the water and carried her away. She felt everything, but she couldn't see it. She couldn't respond and she couldn't move. She was still choking, but it slowly went away when someone placed her on a bed and kissed her head. Then she stopped feeling. She stopped hearing and she fell asleep again.

She woke up in a large bright room. Torches lit in a large chandelier on the ceiling were casting shadows around the room. Jade sat up and looked around. She was sitting on a large bed full of pillows and blankets. Next to her, there was a table with some blue flowers. They smelled amazing. She was dressed in a white tunic, similar to the one she had gotten in the hospital. The room was painted white with all sorts of blue patterns painted on it. It looked beautiful. A large indigo blue rug was covering the wooden floor. She stood from her bed. The floor was cold. On the other side of the room, there was a table. Neatly arranged soaps and scented perfumes were scattered all over it. Next to it, there was a door. Jade slowly pulled the knob and it opened. She entered a room full of clothes. There was every dress a person could imagine. From a simple grown to a masterpiece for a ball to military-styled outfits. She looked at every single one of them. A grey and silver suit caught her attention. It was simple, yet stunning. The upper part was covered in white crystals in the front. They faded out when they approached the back. The back was naked, covered only by a thin silk gown hanging from the shoulders. The lower part was grey. A silk dark blue lace

Wasteland

was covering it in a slow wave falling from the left side. It looked
amazing. Jade stepped in front of a mirror and almost gasped. She
never looked that beautiful in her life before. She picked dark blue
shoes that wrapped around her legs like ballet slippers. Next, she
browsed through-what looked- an endless drawer or jewelry. She
picked up a headpiece. It was made of blue and white crystals and
pearls. It covered her forehead and silver hair like a reverse, hanging crown. She couldn't move her eyes away from the mirror. She
was beautiful. She looked stunning. her eyes stopped on the shining
metalic hand. She almost looked like a machine. It made her sad
but she had no time to waste.

After some time she walked out and opened another door. The
sweet smell filled her nostrils. It smelled of butter. In front of her,
there was a table full of food. Croissants, meat, potatoes. She rec-
ognized those, but the others were unknown to her. The room was
empty and there was a note on the plate.

„Come outside when you're ready." She smiled and sat down. She
didn´t question the weird situation. She deserved to eat. She was
starving for so long. She loaded her plate with all sorts of delicious
food and devoured it until she was more than full.

CHAPTER 23

The Reunion of Hearts

CHAPTER 23: The Reunion of Hearts

Envy walked to the door and slowly peeked in the hallway. A red rug was covering the stone floor and dark wooden bars were supporting the ceiling. A young man approached. He looked like a guard.

„Where are we?" she asked.

„You are in Keywe center." Replied the man. He had long blond hair and piercing bright green eyes.

„We shall leave now. They are waiting." He announced and offered Jade his hand. She took it and they walked through long hallways and large halls to a huge chamber. With every step they took the would around them changed. The stone hallways turned into white, sterile corridors overrun with blue patterns that had liquid flowing through them.

„Pretty neat simulation isn´t it?" Asked the guar without turning to her.

„It´s stunning." sighed Jade in awe. They entered an unimaginably large chamber. Jade slowly started to realize what was happening. She was in Weyn. In the magic world. Except it wasn't magic. It was all technology. The guard took her to the end of the room and crossed his chest with his arms looking at the huge blue symbol drawn across the wall in front of them. She followed his gesture and a voice from behind them laughed.

„You don't need to do that dear. We should be thanking you." Jade looked at her. The lady had pale skin and long brown hair. Her eyes were black and wide. She was wearing a beautiful blue grown. It had pearls scattered all over it. She was wearing a golden flower crown. Her ears were pointy. She had to be an elf but she just looked so...artifitial.

„We called you here to save us."

„Me?" Jade shook her head in confusion.

„Yes, you. There is more to the story than you know. Osen´s plan is to return to the era of Dowak kingdom. He will rebuild everything from scratch."

„Oh no. We only helped him." The queen nodded.

„It's okay. You didn't know. But we need you to stop him. You have to protect us."

„Who are you anyway?" Envy asked carefully.

„There is so much you don´t know child." The lady looked concerned. But then she continued. „Follow me." Jade obediently followed the lady to another room. Blue lines were running along the side of the wall in pairs and then continued along the floor for a few more feet.

„step on the blue lines." The lady gestured towards the colored stripes. and envy placed her feet directly on top of them. Blue liquid rose from them and wrapped around her feet, fixing her in place. her eyes forced shut and she found herself in front of the building, but years ago. The lady was standing beside her and beautiful plants were growing all around. The lady slowly spoke as they walked through the garden.

„You see...this place was built by Osen´s grandfather a hundred years ago. it is the most technologically advanced ever established. Years and years of research happened here. The main plan was to build artificial intelligence to fight in the war and the did so. There was just one small mistake. we became too self-aware."

„You...work for Osen?" jade shook in fear.

„No. let me finish." The lady stopped her immediately. „After we gained consciousness we saw that Osen and his family were in the wrong. We had to fight against it but we had no access to the outside world...That was until you came along." Jade´s stomach twisted. But she kept listening.

„You were made by Osen´s father to become the strongest fighting machine ever created. You were a test subject. A trial. Everything was a setup. a family raised you until you were old enough to get harvested. That´s when you were placed under Arvas´s guidance."

„But...why would my foster parents let that happen."

„They didn't." The lady hesitated for a moment. „They tried to hide you and got executed on the spot. There is no place for mercy in Osen´s army." Jade clenched her fist. Her whole world had

Wasteland

been turned upside down in a matter of minutes. She didn´t know who she was anymore.

„How many of my kind are out there?"

„Just you…Osen realized you were too dangerous to be controlled and had a mindset of your own. We need you to help us defeat him and Arvas too."

„But how can I do that." Jade felt burning rage in her chest.

„With your hybrid powers. You have so much potential. you were created to kill."

„ I never knew." Jade's mind was racing all over the place.

„It's okay dear. Take this for protection." The lady stood up and handed her a small ring on a necklace. „This will remind you that you have your own will. Osen will try to use it against you but you can´t give up."

„But can I come back here?" Jade's eyes frowned.

„Sadly, you cannot. They know you are here and will do anything to capture you." The lady smiled and stretched out her hand. Before Jade could say anything she continued.

„remember Jade…You´re not just a machine. And your friend will be there for you always." She touched her head and the world wrapped before her eyes.

Jade slowly opened her eyes. She was lying on the beach. Her lungs hurt and her vision was blurry. Was it real? It had to be. It felt real. Her mind was spinning around all the questions. She put her hand to her chest to cough. There was a hard object under her white tunic. A ring on a necklace. It WAS real. She thought to herself. What friend was the queen talking about?

Jade stood up and turned around. Emotions overwhelmed her. She was just a killing machine. Made to destroy and end lives. She´ll never be human. She was a disgrace to this world. A loud scream tore from her throat and spilled across the vast valley of red dust. Far in the distance, she saw a figure. It was fragile and slim. She started walking towards it. Then she started running. The white shirt was loosely flowing around her body. With every step she took, a large cloud of dust filled the air. She was now sprinting across- what seemed- an endless ocean of dust, gasping for air. She was close enough now. She stopped and stared. Tears filled her eyes and uncontrollably ran down her cheeks. The grey eyes. The blond hair. The same spark. Yes, it was him. It was love!

„Dust!" She screamed, almost cried out and threw herself into his fragile arms.

The End

Acknowledgments

Over the past two years and a half, my first book went from inception to pages. It was exciting and emotional but most importantly very difficult. I want to thank many people I couldn´t have done it without.

A big thank you to Suzanne Collins and Sarah J. Mass for inspiring me with their amazing work.

I want to thank my parents for all the support and help to get the book published. Without you, this book would never see the light of day.

Thank you to Wais for helping me lecture my book.

I also want to thank everyone who took their time to review my book. You are all awesome inspiring people and I'm thankful for all the support.

I'm grateful for every supportive word from my friends, classmates and others. You believed in me when things weren´t going my way and inspired me to keep going and follow my dreams.

Last but not least, thank YOU for taking your time to read my book.

I´ll never be able to fit everyone I want to thank within this space but I am grateful to every individual who contributed to this book being made. I could never thank you all enough.

THANK YOU.